KASH

A NOVEL

Kimberly Fields

KASH : a novel / Kimberly Fields

Unbounded Creations Publishing Housing

Paperback Original

Copyright © 2016 Kimberly Fields

Published in the United States by Unbounded Creations Publishing House

ISBN- 978-0-692-95021-0

Printed in the United States of America

Publisher / Editor: Kimberly Fields

www.womenalty.com
womenalty@gmail.com

I dedicate this book to my Husband. A natural born hustler.

&

To my children. I do it all for you kings.

KASH

A NOVEL

Kimberly Fields

PROLOGUE

Sup world, what it do? That's my greeting from deep inside the depths of the Federal Correction Institute of Waseca. How and why am I here might you ask? Well, I'll explain that to you later, but first, let me introduce myself.

My government name is Keisha Jefferson, and I go by Kash in the streets. That name has come to be known by many men and women. And when these bastards unleash this woman that they branded a beast, free me from this hell hole, it will be known by many more. Yes, I'm a women, and I plan on making this name roll off the tongues of many when I am free and able to do what I do best. And that's hustle. Everybody know the there is an ugly side to the game. I have been told by my grandmother that, "Cash is the root of all evil." Now me, I am far from daddy's little angel, but I have been known to show love to people. I took care of them, and they showed me love and respect in return. Now you might

1

say that a chick who receives so much love and respect can't be all that bad. Well, as I said, I'm no angel.

On many occasions, I've been described as being evil and downright dirty. Classified as a thug. Ha! When I first heard that, it was funny to me. I am a woman, a feminine, sexy, beautiful woman. While most bitches were out playing the role of a woman to these no life niggas portraying to be like Italians dons they saw on TV or getting their "How to be a thug" instructions from the latest rap videos. I was out here getting it and playing the game in real life. And believe me when I say that when I played the game, I played it for keeps. The things I have done out here in this cruel world to survive were to eat and stay my ass alive.

This was never my dream, living hood rich. I have been just applying my hood survival tactics, and by doing so, I created a monster in the process. So tell me, are you interested so far? Do you want to know more about me? Where I've been and where I'm going? Well sit back and let me whisper in your ear for a minute. Let me take you to the beginning

CURIOSITY KILLS

CHAPTER 1.

I was the second daughter of Shanice Taylor and Kaymar Jefferson. Born on March 5th, 1985 at Hennepin County Medical Center. My mother always told me that I practically killed her when she gave birth to me. She made sure I was the last one of the flock.

My mom was a rich caramel brown skin woman. She had the most radiant smile, deep brown freckles across her button nose and strong cheekbones. There was no doubt why my dad knocked her up as rapidly as he did.

Daddy worked a late night shift at the Union Pacific as Supervisor in Saint Paul. They weren't able to get ahold of him to make it for my birth. And even though my dad wasn't able to make it, the most amazing woman in the universe was there as a backup, my grandma. Ms. Beatrice Taylor. A tall, thin, seasoned, woman who carried Christ in her soul and loved me to the moon and back. I was grannies baby. My sister, Kaylin, was six years old at the time of my birth. She was just excited to be getting a brother or sister and would soon to be a special woman to love me during my lifetime.

These are the women who happen to be responsible for molding and shaping me into the spoiled woman that I have grown to be. Now as you can see, I didn't say anything at all about my daddy spoiling me like his little princess. That's because I never got to know him. He was killed about five months after I was born.

Kaymar was a tall man. Light skinned complexion with a strong muscular built from so many years of hard work. To make ends meet, he sold green on the side. Daddy was the weed man, but he ensured that his nine to five came first. Whatever daddy made off the weed was extra money and believe me, with my mother and her high maintenance lifestyle. He needed all the extra money he could get. It was his fault that she was the way she was. He loved to spoil the most important women in his life. Nothing but the best for his ladies. He created heaven for his angels.

Daddy set high standards for mama. Although I say mama was the one who killed him. She didn't drive the blade that killed him, but she might as well have. Around the time I was born, my daddy started making significant moves in the streets with his weed. Soon, he switched up to a bigger and better connect. A Jamaican who went by the name Rojay.

With the new plug, things were great, business was advancing, and it was all working out. Except for one unexpected wrinkle that my father never saw coming. Rojay had eyes for my mother. He earned the trust of my daddy and was allowed into our home. That was something no other man had the privilege to do.

My mama had quickly gained her shape back after my birth. They say she was more attractive than before. Her hair had grown thick and long. Her skin glowed with radiance as if the sun had kissed her. Mama lived a sheltered life, first with my granddaddy then my daddy. The attention that was being given to my mama by Rojay when my father wasn't looking was something intriguing and exciting to her. The more he did, the more she wanted to explore the possibilities of this strange exotic man from another country showing her this kind of attention. It made her feel special in ways that she never imagined.

On one particular day, my daddy was at home waiting for Rojay to deliver a package of some new weed that he had just gotten in. My sister and I were at my grandma's to not be in the way. My mama and daddy always sampled the new product, and as they were waiting, the Union called asking my daddy to come in because they had an emergency. So my daddy had to go to work. The benefits of being a supervisor. Before he left, my daddy instructed mama to get the package, give Rojay the money and tell him he would call him later. Mama obediently agreed, kissed and hugged daddy as he left. Soon after daddy pulled off, Rojay showed up. He approached mama as she stood in the doorway.

"I'm supposed to pay for the package, and he'll call you later."

"Kaymar not 'ere mon? We're him be?"

"He got a called into work on an emergency," mama replied as she stared transfixed into the man's eyes, wondering why she couldn't look away. It was like she was hypnotized. They say Jamaicans know voodoo.

"So you be 'ere alone woman?"

"Y-Y-Y-Yes," she stuttered out, aroused with desire.

"How 'bout a sample Ganja?" he asked pulling out a pinky size joint.

"O-O-Okay," she uttered, unsure why as she inhaled his sweet scent.

They sat at the kitchen table, sparked the joint and passed it back and forth. Mostly back to mama, after the second joint mama was high as a Georgia pine. Seeing this as his opportunity, Rojay moved in to capitalize.

"Do you want a charge?"

Smiling and high, she answered "Yeah sure."

Rojay placed the joint backward all the way into his mouth and got on his knees between her legs while putting his hands on her lower thighs. She tensed but didn't move. As the smoke started to flow slowly from his mouth and into her hers, he inched his hand up her thighs slowly lifting her floral dress higher and higher. She became excited by this slick and bold move and didn't protest his advances.

Rojay begin kissing her on the lips, as one hand found its way between her legs. Gently stroking her pulsating vagina, while the other was fondling her breast through the sheer fabric of her dress. He paused to take the joint from his mouth and placed it into the ashtray, just as her head fell backwards, lost in ecstasy.

Rojay removed his hand from her breast and grabbed a hand full of her long thick hair. He yanked her head back forcefully, planting a strong lustful kiss on her as his tongue found its way into her mouth.

He had his other hand up under her dress, inside of her panties, which were wet with desire. He fingered her with his middle finger as she moaned out in pure delight. Standing in one sweeping motion, Rojay cleared the kitchen table. He then laid her on top of it and ripped her panties off with a firm yank. He quickly buried his head between her thighs, tasting all of her sweet nectar.

She moaned and screamed out in pure ecstasy, guiding his head as she gyrated her hips, grinding into his face. She could feel herself on the verge of cumming.

"I'm about to cum! I'm about to cum," she panted out.

Rojay stood up and quickly started to unbuckle his pants.

"Not yet woman!"

Just as he unzipped his pants, my daddy stepped through the kitchen door calling out for my mama. "Shanice, I'm home babe. It was…just … a…false… alarm…" He couldn't believe his eyes. His wife was lying half naked on the kitchen table. Legs spread wide open, dress up around her waist with Rojay standing over her, hard dick in hand about to penetrate her.

Pain, hurt, anger, rage…all of these emotions flowing through my daddy at this time. With a clinched fist and gritted teeth he asks, "Nigga what the fuck you doing with my wife?"

Rojay put his dick back in his pants, and mama rolled off the table onto the floor filled with fear. "Kaymar!" She screams out to my daddy as he charged into the Jamaican, swinging with all of the power and strength that he could muster. He swung and missed several times because of the swiftness of the fearful Jamaican.

By this time my mother was huddled up in the corner of the kitchen while my daddy chased Rojay around the kitchen table. Enraged even more by the chase, my daddy overturned the table letting it fly on top of my mother. Kaymar charged the Jamaican and connected with a vicious uppercut that sent him flying out of the kitchen door and onto the back steps. Rojay rolled to the ground. Quickly got to his feet and staggered away towards the front of the house to his car.

Just as the Jamaican reached his vehicle, Kaymar caught him in the back of the head with another blow that sent him crashing into his car. Seeing my daddy coming, Rojay back kicked him in the stomach. This gave him just enough time to open the car door. He made it inside and locked the door.

Kaymar quickly made it back to his feet and tried to get the vehicle door open. He ran around to the passenger side, which Rojay had forgotten to lock and snatched it open.

Shocked and afraid for his life, Rojay reached under the seat for the switchblade that he kept for protection. Taking several blows before he was able to retrieve it. He flicked it open and widely plunged it into Kaymar's forearm, ripping muscle and tissue causing blood to squirt throughout the interior of the car.

The pain hit hard, but this didn't stop Kaymar, he was so filled with anger and rage that he didn't feel it. Well not until Rojay had plunged the blade a second time deep into his upper stomach, the tip of the blade penetrating Kaymar's heart. In fear, Rojay drove the blade in as deep as he could with as much strength as he had and twisted it hard to the right then the left.

Kaymar was halted by confusion and pain as he realized his fate. As his weight fell upon Rojay, thoughts of death crossed through Kaymar's mind, he could see the faces of his children. "Who's going to take care of my babies? My two beautiful children, why did Shanice betray me? I gave her all of my love and more. Why God? Why?" Now it was too late. Everything went black, and he took his last breath. Rojay pushed Kaymar's body over into the passenger seat. Reaching over him, he pulled the door closed, found his keys and cranked the car up and pulled off in a panicky, paranoid state. That was the last anyone had seen of Kaymar until his body turned up several weeks later in Powderhorn Park.

Rojay was found dead a couple of years later in a motel room in Chicago. He had died of a heroin overdose. My guess was that the guilt of my daddy's murder was too much for him to bear.

Now that's how my mama killed my daddy, with her selfish, unfaithful desires. She never was the same again after that night. She stayed high to escape the guilt that was eating her up inside. One drug led to another, and eventually, she found herself a full-fledged crack head.

FIGHTING FOR LOVE

CHAPTER 2.

My youth years were spent dealing with the trials and tribulations of having a crack head for a mother. I know you can relate to what I'm talking about, like the saying goes, "A crack head, there's one in every family."

Despite mama debilitating habit, she would maintain her beauty. She could look just as bad as the rest of them, but most of the time, she kept herself up. Mama had never considered herself being a crack head or even accepted the fact that she had an addiction. I guess that's what the psychologist called "denial." The inability to accept the truth.

Mama maintained her shape and could catch the eye of just about any man. That's how she cared for us growing up, through her sugar daddies. She was even in denial about her whorish lifestyle. It was just another hustle for her. When she was between men and on one of her binges, my sister and

I couldn't stand my mother ways anymore. We would stay with our grandmother Beatrice. Grandma was the shining light at the end of our dark tunnel. She was there in our times of need, and when she wasn't, we had each other.

Kaylin was five years older, and she didn't treat me like most big sisters treat their little sisters. I guess that's one reason we got along so well and is more than likely why I love her so much. Lord knows sometimes we had nothing except each other. My memories of childhood were average just like any other kid growing up around my way. Barbie dolls, doll babies, bikes, reading, you know the average.

I can remember going to school my fourth-grade year—I was a loner. I had friends, but I mainly stayed to myself. I guess because I thought differently from the other kids. My thoughts as a child were more advanced well beyond my years. Where most kids were playing with their new electronic games, I was taking mine apart trying to figure out how they worked. Most children were concerned with eating penny candy, and I was the one supplying it to them at school, jacking up the price to a nickel. I had figured out marketing strategies way back then. I like to think it was my destiny to be a hustler. My mama ran her sugar daddy's, working as a hostess at a restaurant where she met most of them. All while boosting clothes on the side for the extra income. Kaylin, and I were always dressed in the latest gear, which is what brings me to this never forgotten, incident. I was at school on lunch break when a group of kids from the projects started with me by calling my mother a whore and a thief. They teased they knew she stole out of the stores and had all these different boyfriends. The leader of the little girls was Stacy. She honestly didn't like me. I presume it was more due to jealousy and envy than anything else. Stacy was always dusty and dressed raggedy, and I was always so fresh and clean. I kept money in my pocket from my candy sells, and Stacy didn't. I did nothing to draw all of the unwanted attention to myself, and she had to act an ass to get it.

On this particular day, it all came to a head. I was fed up with being taunted by Stacy. Usually, I would ignore her, but this particular day neither of us would let it ride. When she said what she said about my mother, I came back with a quick and nasty rebuke.

"You just mad cause after them five dicks your mama sucked last night. She still couldn't buy you nothing but them cheap ass Everlast shoes," I said.

As everyone stood around and looked down at Stacy dusty Everlast shoes with a million scuff marks and a hole on the side. They all burst out into laughter. Stunned by my remark and unable to think of a snappy reply Stacy's anger grew instantly with her embarrassment. With a clenched fist, red face, Stacy charge towards me intending on beating me silly. But I stepped aside at the last moment and stuck my leg out tripping her. She fell hard, face first into the dirt. Everybody laughed even louder than they did the first time. Stacy was on her hands and knees. Starting to get up when I kicked her in the butt causing her to fall face first tasting a mouth full of dirt again. This really got the crowd going. Stacy was beyond angry as she rolled over onto her back and looked up at me. That's when she hollered at the other girls, you clowns better stop laughing and get her. Before I knew it four of them had surrounded me and grabbed me. None of them hit me though. I think they were scared but divided between their fear of Stacy and me. They held me until she got to her feet.

"So you want to talk about my mama, huh? You little punk" Stacy spat.

"Fuck you and your mama!"

That's when she unleashed on me, pounding on my face and stomach as I struggled to get free from the four holding me. After she had knocked the wind out of me, I fell helplessly to the ground beaten and hurt. Stacy stood over me with an evil grin on her face and kicked me in my stomach with all of her strength. It felt like a Mack truck had hit me.

Stacy started raking the bottom of her raggedy shoes across my brand new Jordan's. "Who got the raggedy shoes now?" she asks laughing at her work.

With all the strength that I could muster, I raised my head and yelled your mama bitch. That's when she lost it and started stomping me with no mercy. I just knew it was over for me. Then out of know where the help came. In the form of Tianna Wagner. She came through the crowd and shoved Stacy to the ground.

"That's enough, raise up off her."

Stacy stood up quickly and got up in Tianna's face. Staring her in the eyes, Stacy thought about the reputation she had for fighting. Stacy thought again about retaliating against her. Backing away, Stacy said, "This shit ain't over little girl."

She turned toward her four followers. Come on let's go. Turning to the crowd, Tianna frowned and hollered, "What are you all looking at. Get the hell from around here!" The crowd quickly dispersed, not wanting any part of Tia. She stuck her hand out to help me get up from the ground. "You alright girl?"

"I'm good."

"You don't look like you good."

"I'm good. I got to get home," as I told her fighting back tears of pain.

"Well, school don't let out till three pm and it's just eleven."

"I'm leaving now." I replied holding my stomach and limping off. Tia stood there staring at me, shaking her head. I stopped and looked back, "I don't know why you helped me, but thank you.

"We cool," was her reply. As soon as I got off the campus and out of sight, I took off full speed and ran all the way home crying. As the tears fell, all I could think about was getting home to the comforting arms of my mother so she could ease my pain.

When I got to the house, I was out of breath. I ran through the front door and straight into mama's room without knocking. She was there trying to sleep off the effects of one of her all night drug sessions. I rushed to the side of her bed crying, shaking her awake. "Mama, Mama!"

"Girl, what's wrong with you?" She asked as she groggily arose wondering what was going on.

Through my sobs, I was barely audible, but I stood there and proceeded to tell her what had happened. Mama checked the time on her bedside clock and frowned up angrily at me. Hurt and somewhat still in pain—I was expecting sympathy and compassion. Instead, there was no pity in those furious eyes peering at me. In one swift motion, mama slung the covers off her, exposing a pink satin nightie and grabbed me by my arm as she got out of the bed. Drawing back, raising her hand high in the air, she came down with a powerful slap across my face that made my knees buckle. Jerking my face up towards her, she spoke sharply. "You mean to tell me you came running your ass in here waking me up for that bullish? You better get your ass back to that school and whip that girl ass or else when you get back home—I'm gone beat yours." She then threw me into the wall and yelled, "Now get your ass up out of here?"

Stunned by what had just taken place, I stood there dumb founded, not knowing what to think or do. But I was quickly brought out of my daze when I ducked to dodge a piece of brass that she threw at me. "You can't hear? Get the fuck out!"

Walking back to school. I was hurt by my mama actions. I wanted to earn her approval by going back and kicking the shit out of Stacy ass. I stopped in the abandoned lot that was overgrown with weeds and trees to collect myself. I had to figure out exactly what I was going to do. I decided to wait until school was out, so I wouldn't get in trouble with any teachers for cutting class. Not only that but it gave me the upper hand. Stacy wouldn't be expecting me to retaliate so soon. Lying in the bushes down the street from the school, I waited for my time to strike. I would be able to hear the bell and the other kids when they came out.

At three pm the bell rang, and I got ready. I waited for my prey anxiously. I knew the route that Stacy had to walk, so I was in the right place. Peeking through the bushes, I saw a lot of kids passing. None of them even notice me. I watched a few more kids walk bye. There she was. Stacy was walking with two of the girls that helped her earlier. Seeing the other two girls, I knew that my chances had dramatically lessened because of their presence. I thought quickly of a contingency plan. I cursed myself for not thinking of this problem earlier. As my mind raced. I thought my plan of retaliation was at a lost until I looked down and saw a thick branch that had fallen from one of the trees. I picked it up and tested the weight with a few practice swings. Now I was ready.

I emerged from the bushes with nothing on my mind but beating the living hell out of Stacy. The limb was half hidden behind my back as I approached her. She started laughing with the other girls when she saw me.

"Look, it's that little clown Keisha. Girl I told you I was gone get you, now I'm gone fuck you up."

Without warning or even a single word uttered, I swung the branch with all of my might. I struck her in the left arm.

All the others kids scattered out the way. Wielding the stick like Ken Griffey Jr. The two girls with Stacy now stood back with fear and amazement in their face. I continued to strike Stacy, hitting her all over her body as she cried and screamed for her mama. As I swung, she tried to block the blows with her arm and hands. By now a crowd had formed around us and was screaming and egging me on.

"Get her! Get her! Get her!" They chanted. I had slipped into a zone. Unable to hear anything or anyone. The only focus in mind was the destruction of Stacy. At least until I was bear hugged behind by Tianna. She had my arms as she pulled me away.

Snapping back to reality, I let the limp drop to the ground. I looked at Stacy, and she was crying and covered in blood. I knew I had gone too far. That's when I noticed the police officer that patrolled the school, running towards the crowd. "What you kids doing?" screamed as approached. Scared and in a state of panic, I stood there staring back and forth between the cop and Stacy. Tia pushed me in my back and screamed "Run Keisha, run!" hearing her words I shot out like a streak of lighting. Running down the street, I came to the intersection at the end of the block but didn't see the pickup truck until it was too late. It hit me head on. That was the last thing I remembered.

MOOD

CHAPTER 3.

I woke up several days later in the hospital. Grandma and my sister Kaylin were standing over me smiling. I tried to adjust my eyes to the light. "Thank you Jesus! Thank you Jesus! Thank you Jesus!" My grandma said praising the Lord. I looked down at my body and could see that most of it was covered in a cast. Suddenly remembering what had happened, I managed to form a few words in my mouth. "Where is mama?"

From the looks exchanged between Grandma and my sister, I knew that my mother wasn't there and probably hadn't been. My grandma was the one to answer.

"Well," she started, "your mama had some business to take care of Keisha. But she'll be here."

Everyone in the room knew it was a lie. The look on Kaylin's face as she rolled her eyes at grandma's words, told it all. I turned my head and let tears fall. Right then and there is when I promise myself that this would be the last time that I ever cried over the lack of love that I received from my mother. She wasn't a mother to me anymore. She was simply Shanice. And from that day on, I referred to her as much. My recovery was bad but not as bad as one would have thought. I went to my grandma's house to recover. Kaylin and I moved in for a while. After the lack of love displayed by Shanice during my hospital stay. Grandma thought it was best that we stayed with her. I'm sure my daddy would have wanted it that way.

Kaylin and grandma really stuck by me during this time and afterwards. I believed for Kaylin, the thought of losing her only sister brought us closer to one another. This gave grandma the opportunity to spoil us even more than she already had. Tianna came to the hospital during my recovery stage. She had showed up to talk to me until vising hours ended. She kept me in the loop on what was going on in the hood. Plus she said she had taken over my penny candy operation for me, but profits weren't what she had expected. I gave her the game on how to make the change, and she faithfully followed. She also brought me two piggy banks full of nickels a couple of months later. Telling me that it was my half of our business. Over the years Tianna and I became best friends. When Kaylin and I move back in with Shanice, Tianna house became my third home. My grandmothers being my second one, and truthfully I don't even know if I would had call Shanice house my home. I was barely there plus the house was void of love. The only love there was the love that Kaylin, and I shared. During our time in Minneapolis, we lived on the corner of 33rd street and 3rd Avenue, Central neighborhood. The south side of Minneapolis. My grandmother lived not far from us in the same neighborhood off of 38th street and 2nd Avenue.

Grandma said that she stayed close so she wouldn't have far to come to get on her nerves and run her crazy. Whatever the reason may have been, Kaylin and I was glad to be in close proximity to grandma house.

Central was always beefing with other neighborhoods and sides of towns. I sat back and watch this throughout my years of growing up. Some of us younger kids got into the beefs at times. Tianna and I stayed away from it, but I can't say the same for Kaylin. She was a very beautiful young lady. Back then she got hit on by a lot of older guys. That in turn brought on a lot of envy and jealousy from a lot of females. Kaylin road with a click of females that she was the self-proclaimed leader of called the Southside girls. They fought, stole, partied, and did just about whatever they wanted to do.

Grandma used to make sure that she kept us in church every Sunday but after she found out that Kaylin was in a gang, the church services for us increase from just Sunday morning services to Sunday night service, and Wednesday night revival. I guess this was grandma's way of trying to get the Lord to save Kaylin from the streets. Every time grandma would confront Kaylin, she would always deny the existence of a gang and say that they were simply her girlfriends that she studied and hung out with. Grandma would accept the answer not believing in it. She would mention to Kaylin. "Kaylin Jefferson, you can lie to me, but you can't lie to the good Lord and God don't like ugly."

Kaylin would write off her words and keep doing what she did. We love our grandma, and we knew she loved us. We always respected her and never wanted to disappoint her. Kaylin and I figured that she had just lost track of how things were in this day and age.

During these years Kaylin started gaining her popularity and by me being her little sister, I received a lot of attention myself. I really didn't care for it though. The only thing I wanted to do was kick it with my girl Tianna and ride our bikes all day. We still had our candy hustle going, but we wanted more, so we started stealing bicycles from the kids in the Nokomis area. Our base of operations was Shanice's house she rarely went out back, plus I knew she didn't really care what I did anyway. As long as I didn't bother her.

Looking back on my life, those were my happier years. I had somewhat of a loving family. A stable environment that I knew, and loved. That was until Shanice met a drug dealer from Los Angeles, California named Richard Adams. A well-known drug trafficker. Shanice thought she was in love, but I knew that it was the daily rotation of drugs that Richard was giving her that she was in love with. Not the man himself.

Rich was cool, like Kaylin and I a lot, but when convinced Shanice to move to California with him and to bring us along. I was highly mortified. How could I leave the only place I've ever known? How could I leave Tianna and grandma just to go to some crazy city? I can remember the night before we left. We stayed over to our grandmas—she prepared a great big dinner with all of Kaylin's and my favorite foods. Grandma even told us not to worry about the dishes after dinner. She called us into her bedroom and told us to have a seat on her bed so she could talk to us.

"Now girls," she began. "I know you're going to that big city but don't never forget your grandma is nothing but a phone call away all right," she started trying to hide her sadness.

"Yes ma'am," we replied in unison.

"Now your mama ain't too bright upstairs sometimes when she on that stuff, but y'all already know that. Just look out for her best interest. I know she does some messed up stuff, but she's still my daughter and y'all mama. All we can do is pray for her, and ourselves. Now y'all get on your knees so we can pray one last time together."

Obediently we got on our knees to pray with grandma. It almost seemed surreal. This could be the last time the three of us prayed or even shared a meal together. How awkward indeed, unable to get on my bike and go see my grandma. Grandma grabbed both of our hands, gripping them tightly— she bowed her head and closed her eyes as she began to pray.

"Father God in heaven, I ask for your mercy, kindness, and for your forgiveness. We come to you with all degree of humbleness, asking you to walk with us through these up and coming times. I ask that you look after these two babies here and don't let no harm come their way." As grandma prayed, I held my eyes closed tight. I was already missing her. "I pray for their mother too. We done had many a prayer sessions we can about that child of mine. Lord, I'm praying extra hard for her now. So she can have common sense, strength and a loving heart to do what is best for my grandbabies. Keep them close to you Lord, and keep them from harm's way. If it is your will, let them find their way back to these loving arms of they're grandma. In Jesus heavenly name, Amen."

We all said Amen along with grandma, and when we all lifted our heads, we were on the verge of tears. It was one of the most endearing and tender moments of my life. Grandma squeezed our hands and gave us a faint smile, letting us know that things were going to be alright. Then slowly stood.

"Now, I got something for y'all. Have a seat on da bed," she said and went to her closet. Grandma rummaged through the shoeboxes on the floor and came out with a non-descripted blue box. She brought it over to the bed, opening it and pulling out two envelopes. She handed them to Kaylin.

"Kaylin, in these envelopes, you gone fine five hundred dollars in cash and two one way bus tickets going from California to Minneapolis. Now, this money is just in case things get bad on y'all and y'all needs it. It isn't for you to run your butt to the store buying up everything. And these tickets is for you and your sister to get back home to me if that bad day ever arises. Kaylin, if your grandma have never asked anything of you in your life, it's now that I need you to be a woman. A woman who can handle responsibilities because it isn't all about you when you make it way out there to the big city. It's about Keisha as well. It's about family."

"I'm a big girl grandma—I can take care of myself," I interjected.

Grandma patted me on my knee and gently replied. "I know you can baby, buy y'all stand a better chance if you stick together. You see, that's what family is supposed to do. Stick together. No matter what. You hear me? No matter what!" She said staring between us. Now, Kaylin, I need you to make me this promise before God and me right now. Are you willing?"

"Yes ma'am, Kaylin replied with anxiety and fear in her voice. Grandma started again.

"Promise God, and me that you will always be there for your sister, never letting anything or anyone harm her and that you will defend her until your last breath. Because one day, me and your mother might not be around. So let me hear you girl."

"I promise Grandma, on Kaymar Jefferson grave," Kaylin stated with newfound conviction and strength. Grandma turned to me and said, "and you young lady, do you here promise to do the same by your sister?"

"Yes Ma'am. I promise and may God strike me down if I am lying."

Right then and there I could feel the love and commitment of that eternal oath that we were partaking in. We all felt it and meant it. I thought to myself—now this is what family love is supposed to be.

Later that night, I was in my room at grandmas, when I heard someone tapping on the window. I drew back the curtain to see Tia white teeth smiling at me. That's all I could see because Tia was black as tar. I opened up the window, and she stuck her face in.

"What's up Keisha, you coming out so I can holla at you?"

I smiled and said, "yeah if you move your black butt out the way so I can climb out."

She started laughing, and I quickly shushed her. "Shush, girl what are you trying to do, get me in trouble?"

"Man, bring your scary self on out the window," Tia replied still laughing as I climbed out. We walked to our old clubhouse in the back of my grandma's house. Well, actually it was another spot for us to store bikes after we broke them down and rebuilt them at Shanice's house. We were both quiet for a minute—then Tia broke the silence. "So you really leaving huh?"

"Yea, we suppose to leave tomorrow. Richard will be here tomorrow afternoon, then we Cali bound."

"Man, I wish you weren't going. Who am I going to have as a sidekick now? And who am I going to crack on? You know you my duck, don't you?" Tia joked.

We both laughed at then got quiet all of a sudden. We were both trying to say goodbye, but not wanting to at the same time. I was going to miss Tia, my best friend in the whole world and I knew she was going to be missing me just as much.

I looked at Tia and said, "I need a big favor from you."

"What's up?"

"I need you to look after my grandma while I am gone. You think you can handle that?"

"For sure, anything for my best friend. Plus I couldn't let anything happen to Ms. Beatrice—she's like my grandma too."

"Swear to me, Tianna."

"I swear on my life. I'm not going to let anything happen to her. I'll protect her like I would protect you."

At that moment I knew our friendship was real. I hugged Tianna showing my appreciation.

"So you think you coming back?"

"I don't know—you know how crazy Shanice is. If stuff gets crazy though, grandma hit me and Kaylin off with some money and some tickets to come back home."

"Grams be looking out."

"Of course."

"Well, I'm going to head out before my mom wakes up and has a fit that I'm not in the bed," Tia said getting up off the wooden crate to walk out the clubhouse.

"Aight," I said reaching towards Tia to give her one last hug.

Tia walked out the gate. I watched my best friend fade into the darkness just like my life was fading.

FIRST ENCOUNTER

CHAPTER 4.

Los Angeles was huge. I was in awe when we first got there. The traffic, the fast pace, and crowds of people. It all amazed me for the first couple of months—afterwards I viewed it all as if it was where I came from, but bigger. As summer was ending and school starting soon. The anxiety of me starting a new school was making me reluctant to attend. Kaylin wanted to go to get out of the hotel room we were staying in. Richard wasn't big on school, and Shanice didn't care. Just as long as her addiction was satisfied. So that first year Kaylin went to school, and I didn't. But Richard had his own form of education for me. I rode with him to check trap houses. From running my penny candy and selling stolen bikes. saw the hustle in me.

Rich had family here in California. was born and raised. His mother and two sisters were all affiliated with the game in some kind of way. His mother's crib was his number one trap

1

house. As far as brains go, they were as dumb as a box of rocks.

All they knew was hustling. But for the life of me, I couldn't understand how they hustle all day long, and their profits were mediocre. I knew Rich had a mountain of bills from the way we moved from room to room every day. But they all lived poorly, and their houses were roach infested and nasty. I derived that it was just how they lived. Now as far as their elevation in the game, I saw their problem. There was always somebody around, stealing or conning them out their money.

His sisters would run through men like water trying to buy love. As ugly as they were, they had to have a lot of money to convince a man to look past all the ugliness. They let themselves get swindled by men in their lives all the time. I learned a lot from this dysfunctional family. How to hustle, how to scheme, and how not to be a sucker for love.

Another introduction that Rich exposed me to was the foreign connect. One reason Rich stayed in the game was because of his connects. had several, and all of them were Columbian or Puerto Rican. explained they come from where the dope is made, and they have family back home who knows somebody or is somebody. These people sent it to them to distribute, so why score from the middleman who will jack up the prices. When you can get it straight from the source. It all made sense. Who knew Rich old dusty ass had that much brainpower running around in that big head of his. showed me all kinds of love. Treated me as if I was his own and since I took a liking to his business, he gave me whatever I asked for. He and Kaylin were cool, but he took more of a liking to me.

This same monotonous routine of living went on for the next couple of years, except Rich got us a house in Sawtelle, away from his drug dealing. This is when I finally got into a school and was doing very well. I even made up for the year that I missed, and still went everywhere with Rich.

By the age of fourteen, I had filled out into a nice young lady. Many would say I was too advanced. And since I was always with Rich, I had become well known on the streets where he did his business. So many knew my age and to not mess with me. I never actually did business around the spots, but I knew everything there was to know about the business. I had a cool laid-back style for a girl that everybody liked. It was cool here but I wasn't happy, I had missed home. Meanwhile, Kaylin had thrown herself into school and friends. She had met numerous amounts of people while living in Sawtelle. She and Shanice stayed into it about Shanice drug habit and her lack of love when it came to us. Rich would always leave during these arguments and fights. He wanted nothing to do with the drama.

One day things got so bad that my sister packed up all of her stuff and left. She called me later crying, telling me that she couldn't do it anymore and she was staying with some friends and their family. She asks if I wanted to go back to Minnesota with grandma, but I was reluctant to leave her here. We had made an oath to be there for one another. I didn't fault her for moving out. Kaylin was there for me every day and called several times a day. If anything, we got closer. The reason that Kaylin didn't want to leave California and move back to Minnesota was because of her education. She wanted to finish at a top school to afford herself better opportunities when it came to college. After graduating high school, Kaylin earned an academic scholarship to attend UCLA: The University of California, Los Angeles. She majored in pharmaceutical and minored in business, Kaylin was a natural scholar, and learning came easy to her.

At that same time, partying started. Not the wild and loose type of stuff but Kaylin became a regular in the club scene. One night out, she met Mr. Ricardo Pérez, also known as

Rico. Rico, a dark complexion Columbian immigrant, was pretty heavy in the dope game and had a passion for black culture. That's how he and Kaylin met at a black club in South Central LA called The Vault Night Club & Lounge. They hit it off from day one, and Rico was in love from that moment on.

Kaylin played hard to get with him, but it only fueled his already burning desire to possess this black beauty. He lavished Kaylin with all kinds of gifts and would show up outside of her classes and at her dorm room. Kaylin vigorously resisted, but Rico was relentless in his pursuit of her until she finally surrendered to his advances and agreed to be his girl. After their relationship was made official, Rico moved Kaylin into a town home and bought her a car. Even though Kaylin and I talked daily and I saw her a couple of times a week, I still hadn't met Rico. She knew Rico and how he lived and refused to expose me to his world, although I was already mixed in it. Being a pharmaceutical student, Kaylin eased her way into Rico's world and became quite useful. Actually more than useful, she became invaluable. Kaylin lab skills were second to none when it came to cooking and testing the purity of the drugs. My sister never let me in on what she was doing. All I knew was that big sis kept little sis dressed to impress and provided for whatever it was that I needed. Which wasn't much because Rich provided for me as well. Besides what I provided for myself from my earnings on the side.

It was the summer of 2001. I was sixteen years old and life was good. Despite Shanice and her addictive habits. She had become a recluse. People rarely saw her, except Rich. Honestly, I really didn't too much care. It was her life to do with it as she wished. But this particular day, I was rolling with Rich while he checked his spots and picked up his money. Nothing out of the ordinary, just another day. When we pulled up to the house in Compton. This hooker named

Michelle was standing out there. When we got out of the car, she approached us.

"Hey Rich, what's up? Those peoples been rolling hard in unmarked cars today so watch yourself."

"Aight, I'm on the lookout. Appreciate that," Rich told her.

"Fa sho'. Oh, hey, Lil lady."

"What's up," I replied.

I sat in the car while Rich dipped in the house to take care of his business. I had never talked with Michelle before, and my mind was trying to figure out why she was even out here. She was too pretty, yellow bone, tall, thick with a flat stomach with a super model face. But despite all of this natural beauty. She was still out there on the streets doing what she does. As I stared at her, she must have figured out what was on my mind. Michelle burst out into laughter saying,

"You think I'm one of these street walking zombie bitches? Wrong one baby. There's a spot a couple of houses down that we can go to where I can blow your mind. If you can read between the line. So what's up?"

Shocked by her forwardness, I decided to take her up on her offer, and we headed towards the house.

"One of your spots?" I asked.

"I come here sometimes to look out for your step dad dope houses, and he takes care of me for that. We kind of like peoples you know. Keisha, just to let you know, I'm not like these other hoes around here. I don't know what you might or might not have heard about me."

"Oh, why does it matter?"

"You probably don't even care about that anyway. Just come over here and let me taste that love." She whispered.

When I walked over to Michelle, she sat me down in a chair, lifted up my sundress, and then spread my legs. Michelle got down on her knees, lifted one of my legs over her shoulder. Sliding my panties to the side, she placed her lips on mine. She slowly licked my sweetness in a circle motion with her tongue. I slide down in the chair till my ass cheeks were hanging at the edge, and I threw my head back letting out a light moan. With one hand she kept my lips spread apart while her other hand roamed and found its way to my breast. She gently squeezed and pinched my nipples. She was definitely a master at her trade. She had my legs shivering. Michelle continue to lick and suck on my nectar. I could feel myself about to cum, but I wasn't about to let her know that. Yet I knew she already figured it out by the way I started to shake. Michelle, stuck two fingers deep inside me as she continued to suck and lick my kitty. Letting out a moan as I began to let my juices flow while she slurped every trickle. Afterwards, she raised up and looked at me, and smiled. I was weak as hell. She began licking me again, letting out slight moans as talked to me.

"Hmmm you taste so sweet," just then we were disturbed by a loud crash, screaming and the sound of sirens coming from outside, somewhere near like down the street. I jumped up and ran to the window to see what was going on. Cops were everywhere. The majority of them still running inside the dope house where Rich was. I stood in a daze until I felt Michelle tugging on my dress.

"Come on, I know a spot where we can check to see what's going down. You can see this shit was a setup. Ain't no telling if those peoples saw you pull up with Rich when I walked to the car to talk to y'all. So they might be looking for us too," she said.

"Yeah, you right let's roll," I replied following her lead. She took me out back to an alley, down a couple of houses to a hole in a fence where we came out on the next street over. To my surprise, Michelle produced a set of keys to a blue Chevy Caprice that was parked on the block. We hopped in, and she drove us two streets over, back the way we had just come. After Michelle had parked, we got out and crossed through another yard and stepped into another alley, then through somebody's back door without knocking.

I asked, "Who crib this?"

"It's my uncle Mel's house. He's old and sick, plus he in a wheelchair. Your step daddy looks out for him here."

"Why he do that?"

"What?"

"Look out for your uncle?"

"Because girl, I been knowing Rich for years and my uncle use to look out for him back in the day."

Michelle led me into the living room where her uncle was sleeping in his wheel chair. Right in front of the television. We both quietly crept to the window and pulled back the drapes. To my surprise, we were directly in front of Rich's dope house, and there was Rich, in handcuffs, being questioned by several narcotics agents. He had a blank expression on his face like he was in another world.

"Damn! I told Rich ass that them folks were riding around here," Michelle complained.

"This is fucked up Michelle. What you think happened?" I asked.

"Baby Rich been trying to push too much weight around here at super cheap prices. By doing that, he been taking over these other dudes customers, making all the bread."

"So you think it was one of these dudes around here?"

"If I had to guess, yeah."

"Um-hmm."

"So what do you want to do? Do you want to call your mom?"

"Naw, just give me a ride to the south side, and I got ya."

"Baby, you don't have to pay me."

I texted Kaylin. You see, I couldn't let Michelle take me to the crib because nobody knew where we lived and that was a firm rule that was never to be broken. I didn't want her to know what area we stayed in either. That's why I texted Kaylin to come pick me up. I had her stop at an In-N-Out Burger. Kaylin was there in a matter of minutes. When Kaylin was pulling up, and I was getting ready to get out of the car, Michelle touched my arm and spoke. "Keisha?"

"What's up?"

"Look this is my number. I want you to call me if you ever need me or anything. I know this ain't the time or place for all this, but I would really like to see you again. If that's cool with you?" She asked shyly inspecting the big letdown. Skepticism was written all over her face.

"Yeah Michelle, that's cool," I said half smiling.

"Well, can I get your cell number too?"

I thought about it for a second and thought why the hell not.

"Yeah, you can get it."

We exchanged numbers, and I thanked her for the ride. I got in the car with Kaylin and explained to her what just went down and why I had to call her. We headed straight to the house, but not before circling the block a few times to make sure that it was safe. When we made it inside, I started calling Shanice name, but she didn't answer. We checked every room in the house. No Shanice. The phone started to ring. Kaylin answered it.

"Hello." She listened for a second, then turned to me. It's Rich calling from jail" Kaylin accepted the call.

"What's up Rich?"

"Who dis, Kaylin?"

"Who else fool? You know don't nobody, but four people know where this house is at? Keisha called me when things went down."

"Where she at? Is she alright?"

"Let me talk to her."

I grabbed the phone from Kaylin, "What up man?"

"Well, you already know the salt shaken snitched ran to the blue bitches, trying to kill a nigga hopes and dreams."

"Yeah, I know. Ol'girl and I were peeping the scene from Uncle Mel's crib," I told him.

"Well, you did good, and you were in good hands. It's more to her than meets the eye. Keisha she good peoples. Now, where your mama at?"

"You mean, Where Shanice at? I don't know—she wasn't here when we got here."

"Well, let her know what the deal is when she gets back. But Keisha, I need you to do me a big ups. I need you to take charge. It doesn't look like I'm going to get out without a lawyer. These crackers got me labeled as a king-pen. I think the feds might try to snatch me up. Now, I'm going to give you the keys to the kingdom, and I need you to handle it for me, okay?"

"For sure, I got you."

Rich let me know where the money and the drugs were. I was to give all of the drugs to Kaylin. He spoke with her and told her what to do. Kaylin agreed and handed me the phone back.

"Yeah, Rich."

"Well Keisha, I'll be calling the house for you, and hopefully I get to see you and your mother soon. Y'all have more than enough to hold y'all down for a while."

"I" – click! Was I tripping or did I hear a click on the phone like someone was hanging up on the other end? I motioned for Kaylin to go up front and check the phone. She jumped up and ran out the room and down the hallway. She returned a minute later, nodding her head and confirming what I thought to be true. Shanice had snuck into the house and was listening in on our conversation. How much did she hear? Where is she now? Or better yet, where is she on her way too? Rich had been talking, but I hadn't heard a word he said in the past few minutes. I interrupted him and said, "Rich, I think Shanice was just on the other phone listening. Kaylin ran up front and saw her jump in a car leaving."

"Damn," Rich replied. "Keisha get off this phone and get to the spot before your mother does! If not, everything will be gone!"

"I'm out," I said as I hung up the phone. Kaylin and I ran out the house and hopped into her car. Racing across town, all I could do was hope and pray that Shanice didn't mess this up for everybody. Her and her damn habit! You can't trust no crack head.

HIDE & SEEK

CHAPTER 5.

When we got to Rich spot, we rushed inside to uncover the safe wide open with papers and a few bills strewn across the floor. You could see that someone had came and gone in a rush. I looked over to Kaylin.

"We need to find Shanice and try to get some of Rich's money back or else he through."

"I feel you, But Shanice trifling ass could be anywhere in Cali.

"Yeah, but she's going to go to the only spots that she knows, and those places are in the hood."

"We both know the hood, but not like that. If we stand any chances of finding Shanice, we going to need some help."

"Good thinking Kaylin, I know just the person."

After leaving a message for Michelle from not answering my call. She quickly called back. I explained to her that it was imperative that we find Shanice and without question or hesitation, she readily agreed to meet us in the hood to help.

Michelle went to every spot that she could think of that Shanice might be. And all the old places that I knew. But there was no sight of Shanice anywhere. The hours turned into days, and soon we were about sick of the hide and seek game. It had been five days, and I was at home on the phone talking to Rich when the line beeped.

"Hold on Rich, let me answer the other end," I clicked over.

"Hello."

"Keisha, this Michelle, I think I know where your mother is."

"Oh, yeah?" I replied.

"Yeah what you are going to do?"

"Hold on Michelle." I clicked back over to the other line.

"Rich, that's Michelle, and she thinks she knows where Shanice is at, but Kaylin is in school right now."

"Have Michelle to come get you," Rich told me.

"But you said no one is to know where we stay. You breaking the rules now?"

"Keisha, Michelle is family. She's cool—I'll explain it to you later, just get to your mother!"

"Aight, I'm out," I said as I clicked the line back over to Michelle. I gave her the directions to the house and told her to come pick me up.

Michelle came quickly, and we were on our way to the hood. On the way over, I learned that Michelle, like my sister, was a student at UCLA and that she wasn't a crack whore. Michelle didn't do any drugs what so ever. Michelle was simply out there making money to put herself through college, the only way she knew how in the only place she knew, the hood. And little to my knowledge, Michelle wasn't a street trick at all. She only tricked with ballers and older wealthy men from the neighborhood.

Her Uncle Mel had put Rich in the game, and in a deal that went wrong, which was Rich's fault, her uncle Mel had been shot several times and paralyzed. One bullet lodged in his brain, and he was never right again after that.

Michelle's parents were killed in a car accident years ago. She was left to be raised by her uncle. After his misfortune, she turned to the streets that she was raised on.

Yeah, Rich did his part, but he could only do so much. And I guess paying for Michelle's college education was too much. The house that she and Uncle Mel lived in had been paid for, so was the car that she drove, all courtesy of Rich.

Michelle explained that Rich was more like an older cousin than anything else. I learned a lot about Michelle on that ride to the hood, and it made me look at her in a different light. I developed a new form of respect for this young black, beautiful woman. Trying to pull herself out of the harsh ghetto that had made her. Her goal was to get a degree, get away from the hood, and never look back.

I listened as Michelle talked about making something of herself. To her it didn't matter what people around the hood thought of her or how they looked at her, in a few years, she would never see them again anyway. At that moment, Michelle became an essential part of my life. I didn't know or realize it at the time. I finally understood what Rich meant when he said there was more to Michelle than meets the eye.

We arrived at a fleabag motel in the hood that rented regular rooms and kitchenettes out by the week. Michelle got out and asked me to chill while she went and hollered at a maid working the spot. She came back a few minutes later and told me that Shanice was in room 222.

I quickly made my way to room 222 with Michelle following closely behind me. When I got there, I knocked on the door lightly. No answer. I waited, then banged a little harder. No answer again. I tried the knob, and it turned. I started to enter, but Michelle quickly grabbed my arm.

"Hold up Keisha. Baby, you don't know who behind that door," she warned me. Out of her purse she produced a small black twenty-two and handed it to me. I took the gun, nodded my thanks, turned the knob and pushed open the door.

Inside it was dark. The only light was coming from the television. I clicked on the light and called out Shanice name, but got no answer. I walked into the room with the gun extended in front of me. I saw what appeared to be a pair of feet sticking out from the other side of the bed. I quickened my pace to see who it was. As I stood there gazing down at a wide-eyed, very much dead Shanice, I felt almost nothing. I know I should be feeling some type of remorse or some sorrow for this woman who had given birth to me, who was supposed to be my mother. Only one thought ran through my mind.

"Shanice, you poor, pitiful dumb woman." Shanice was lying there between the bed and the wall, on the floor with her crack pipe in her hand. I was assuming she overdosed because of the foam around her mouth. I turned to see Michelle crying, repeating, "Oh my God, Oh my God!" I grabbed her by the shoulders, shook her a little and looked into her eyes.

"Michelle calm down for a minute, I need you. We have to find the dope and money."

"W-w-what?" She stuttered out with wide eyes.

"Michelle! We... have... to...find... the... money and dope!" I said louder and with more force as I shook her a little harder.

"But aren't you going to call the police?"

"Yes Michelle, But who needs that dope and money more? Me or the police?"

She understood my point. Michelle snapped out of it, and we started tossing the small room looking for my only means of getting Rich a lawyer and my money to live. After almost twenty minutes of searching, we found nothing. I walked back over to Shanice, looked down at her and shook my head. After a second, I finally gathered up enough courage to search her. I found nothing. Not even five dollars. The only thing that was left was a few pieces of something that looked like crack, sitting in a saucer on the nightstand.

I looked down at the saucer. From the color of the pebbles, I could tell that it wasn't Rich dope. I picked a piece of it up and held it up to the light. I turned it, trying to get a good look at it.

Michelle joined me and asked, "Keisha, what is it? Let me see it," Michelle said taking the dope between her fingertips. She looked at it with much scrutiny, smelled it, then stuck her tongue out and barely touched the piece of dope. Immediately, she frowned and spat on it the floor.

"Ugh! Keisha, this ain't no dope! It's rat poison!"

"Shit! They probably up in here smoking together, knew she had all that dope and money, and knocked her off for it. That explains why nothings here." I looked at Michelle and shook my head. I walked to the telephone and called the police.

A couple of weeks later, I found myself in front of Shanice gravesite, watching as they lowered her casket into the ground. We had Shanice's body brought back to Minnesota, and we were having her buried at Oak Hill Cemetery in Richfield next to our daddy. Grandma was trying to be strong but was crying up a storm. Kaylin was there hiding behind a pair of big dark shades. And even though we had just met, Michelle came all the way from Cali to be there. A big array of old friends and acquaintances that known Shanice over the years were in attendance. Grandma walked over to where Kaylin, Michelle and I were standing, hugged me and said, "Keisha I got your room ready, so you're coming back home."

"But grandma, what about all my stuff and the things we left in the house?"

"Kaylin can take care of all that and ship it to you. Now I've done said what I had to say, and that's that."

"Yes Ma'am," I submitted

"Perhaps it's for the best Keisha, at least until I finish school."

"Now Kaylin, you know I could come stay with you and Rico, but you don't want me too."

"And there is a reason behind that Keisha, and I'm pretty sure by now you know why. We've never talked about this, and I don't think right now is the time!"

"When will it be a good time for you Kaylin? You know, I don't get you. You say you love me so much. We are supposed to have each other's back one hundred percent. You moved away and started living this top secret life that doesn't include me. That's a funny way of showing your love," I huffed angrily.

"Look Keisha, Rich and Shanice might have had you around that life, but not me! I do love you. What I do for Rico and his people is for the benefit of us. So you don't and won't have to be out here in these streets. Don't you see that I've been trying to protect you?"

"Kaylin you can't protect me. I'm a product of my environment, and if that's the road I wanted to take, I will do it with or without you. You're the one who intended to go to college and live a square life, not me. We are what we are Kaylin, and that's products of the streets."

Kaylin stood there silently with her head down not saying a word. My grandmother had already left after she had spoken her peace.

"Don't trip though Kaylin, I'm going to stay here in Minneapolis. Just send me my stuff," I said.

"Keisha you know I love you," she replied, pulling me into her arms for a big hug. I hugged her back.

"Yeah I know, and I love you too."

I let her go, looked at Michelle and took her by her hand as I walked her to her car. She spoke first.

"So, you just walked into my life and leaving me already?"

"Leaving you?" Hell, I didn't know you cared."

"Come on Keisha—you see I like you a whole hell of a lot. I came way down her for your mother's funeral, didn't I? I know you got your family and all, but I came here to be with you. I can't explain it, but there is something about you that makes me feel alive inside. Something that I've never felt.

I've never had feelings like this for a woman before. And those feelings are for you."

I just stared at her, holding her hands in mine, saying nothing.

"What is it? Am I too old for you? Is it my lifestyle? I don't have to be your girlfriend, just let me be there for you," she said and lowered her head to the ground.

I took my index finger and lifted her head. Looking into her eyes as tears fell from them.

"Baby, you got that." I smiled and hugged her tight as she turned her head into my chest crying even harder.

Through sniffles, she cried, "Thank you," over and over again.

THE COME UP

CHAPTER 6.

Life back in Minneapolis had changed. I was living with grandma and running with Tia, who had become a small time runner for one of the dope boys in the hood. She was also into stealing anything that she could get her hands on if she thought it could make a profit. But soon all of that was about to change. I had brought the stash that I had put away for myself in Cali with me. Which was about ten ounces of crack cocaine and a couple of grand—that I had saved along with some money Kaylin had given me.

It was summer time when I got back, so there was no school. I just sat back and watched everything and everybody. I didn't even let Tia know about my stash, but the time to do something was upon me. The little stash of money I had was going fast, just as quick as the money Kaylin was sending too. Grandma was getting old, the house and her beat up Buick were both in need of much repair. Tia would have things fixed for her when I was in Cali, but she had used old shady mechanics and contractors, who were more than likely on crack. If grandma had known that to be true, they wouldn't have touched anything of hers. During the first month back, I busied myself with the task of making things right. I never knew that repairing a house could get so expensive. Plus, it was the fact that I had gotten used to living a certain way.

By the end of that month, Tia and I were periodically visiting some dudes out in the boondocks that we had met downtown Minneapolis in the nightlife. I notice that a lot of them were d-boys living on the outskirts of the cities, but would come back to the hood to do their dirt. Tia didn't know about my female encounter back in California. Hanging around these guys were more for getting my shit together to re-up. I was hoping to get Kaylin involved so that I could get the dope at a lower price from out of California. I would cross that bridge later, but for now, it was time to get things moving.

From hanging around the guys we met downtown, I met these two sisters. One was eighteen, and the other was sixteen. The eighteen-year-old, Alexis, had a two-year-old son that was never there. And her little sister Ashley was staying there for the summer while school was out. It was government assistance all the way. I was kicking it in their living room watching TV when I had asked Alexis why she didn't have cable or a DVD player. She said, "My job only part time and I be needing the little money I get for this apartment and my baby."

"So what you saying is, these are things that you would like to have but just can't afford?"

"Yeah Keisha, Why? You gone get them for me?"

"I might, but what are you going to do for me?"

"Damn, that bomb ass head I am giving you isn't enough?"

"No," I replied flatly. "Look here—I'm trying to get money, not give it away. But in the process of me getting mine, you can get yours too. But your ass ain't gone be leeching off me—you're going to earn it."

"How?

"I'll tell you but first let me get Tia here." I called Tia to come over—she arrived about ten minutes later.

"Listen up—I got a deal for you. Well, for all of you if you're down." Ashley, Alexi's sister, came walking out the back room.

"What kind of deal and am I included in it?" Ashley asked while taking a seat next to Tia.

"Yes, but I need to know if you down for this. Well, Tia I already know you got me one hundred percent, but it's you two ladies that I am really asking,"

"I want to hear what it is first because I am not stripping or hoeing," Alexis said with attitude.

"Don't flatter yourself, Alexis, this isn't about that. I'm talking about getting some dope money. I've got a plan to make some cash and get everybody paid."

"Excuse me," Tia interrupted, raising her hand as if we were in school and I was the teacher, trying to be funny. "But where are we going to get the work to do all this stuff to get us paid, Mrs. Nino Brown?"

"We don't need to get it, I already have it."

"What? You mean to tell me you been holding out on me? What you got?"

"Not holding out, just peeping the scene first and waiting for the right time to tell you. And as far as how much, it's enough to start us off right."

And so, right there, my life as a drug dealer started. I formulated a plan and explained it to the girls. We would only sell to the up and coming young street hustlers in the hood. Bypassing the fiends because they bring too much heat.

And so it began. The stash was stored at Ashley and Alexis mothers' house—where Alexis son was most of the time. Their mother was a beautiful easy going lady who worked hard and wanted Alexis to learn the same values, but at the same time, she wanted her first and only grandchild to be raised right. That was the reason she took custody of him. In which the house was safe, and Ashley was able to bring as much drugs needed, to school or Alexis house when told. The school was the place where most of our sales went down at midnight every night except weekends. That was due to us knowing that all of the big timers were in the clubs, so that left the street hustlers with nobody to buy from. That's where we came in. We sold fifty dollar flippers, halves, and wholes. The only problem was where we would re-up from.

The first time we re-up it was with a couple of locals, but we pretty much broke even. That's when it hit me, Kaylin! Not dealing with Kaylin directly but through Michelle. I had remained in constant contact with Michelle, and she was planning to come up and kick it with me during her next break.

They say absence makes the heart grow fonder, in Michelle's and my case. Our relationship had grown leaps and bounds. But because I was young and experimenting, I wouldn't let myself go beyond fondness. Michelle thought that she had found the love of her life.

Everything was working out. I put Michelle in contact with Kaylin, saying that she was tired of playing niggas for money and wanted to try her hand in the dope game. Since Rich was gone, it was a lot of money to be made. Kaylin gave Michelle a direct plug straight to Rico since she considered Michelle people by way of Rich. Once Michelle got hold of the product. I would board a bus with Alexis and shoot to California, where Michelle would pick us up, and we'd take care of business. Both women knew about each other, and I let it be known I didn't belong to anyone of them. They both were into me and played a part in my life, pleased to share time with me. But I would always make time for Michelle to have alone.

Things were going well. Everybody was happy and getting paid. Tia had recruited a couple of youngsters to run for us, but we mostly took care of the business ourselves. Alexis and Ashley went from Dots specials to the top of the line designer's outfits from the best stores in the mall. We thought that things were going well, but in truth, we were slipping big time, about to fall and didn't even know it.

Ashley had an ex name Marcus, who didn't seem to agree with this new found life Ashley was living and getting money. Marcus knew a lot about Alexis and Ashley from being around them all the time. He got with a couple of his older cousins, and they made a plan to rob us.

They had figured out that Ashley was the deliverer. So they watched her every move and saw that she never went anywhere when leaving her mom's house except straight to Alexis when delivering a package. It wasn't hard for them to figure out how to get it.

Hitting the mom's house was too risky, not only due to the area but also because of the burglar bars and the alarm system. They had to get the stash to Alexis house. They waited one night when Alexis was at home alone and knocked on her door asking if she knew the person next door. As soon as she opened the door, they rushed her and quickly bound her with duct tape.

"Look bitch we don't want to hurt you, all we want is the work. We know your little sister got it at your mom's crib. We know because we been watching you and your crew," one of the older cousins mentioned. Apparently the leader of the squad.

"Now all you got to do is call your little sister and tell her Keisha said them peoples are on their way to your mom's crib and that she needs to bring everything over here now. We wait till she gets here, get the dope, then we gone. You understand?"

Staring at the cold eyes behind the black masks, seeing their guns drawn, with fear in her heart and tears running down her face Alexis nodded and replied weakly, "Y-y-yes."

"Good," the leader said. "Now, we gone dial the number for you and you talk," as he motioned to the smaller member of the three man crew. He picked up the phone and started to dial the number as he walked over to Alexis and placed the receiver to her ear and mouth, "And stop that crying shit and talk right bitch."

At that moment it all came together. How did they know her mother's unlisted number and that voice? How could she forget it? She had heard it nearly every day for the past two years. It was Marcus, Ashley's ex. That explained why they knew so much. Suddenly from behind, Alexis felt a large gloved hand wrap tightly around her neck on one side and a cold, sharp knife pressed against her throat on the other side. The crewmember who hadn't spoken whispered harshly into her ear. "Bitch, I'm praying that you fuck this up so I can slice your fucking throat and deliver your ho-ass to your mama in pieces. Remember that."

Ashley picked up the phone on the other end of the line, "Hello," she answered

"Ashley this is Alexis, Um, Keisha called and said them peoples were on the way to moms crib, and you should get everything out of the house now. She wanted you to get everything and bring it over here."

"Why Keisha or Tia didn't call themselves? And why they ain't send no ride for me knowing I don't have one?"

"Look Ashley. I don't know, just do what the fuck I told you to do!"

Ashley knew something was wrong. Alexis never cursed at her for one, and if something like the police was coming to the house, they knew better then to talk about it directly on the phone. Keisha was very adamant about that—She could hear trouble on the line, so she replied, "Okay Alexis, give me a second to get a ride."

"Hurry up!

"Okay be cool, I'm on my way."

Ashley immediately called Keisha. Tia had picked up Keisha's phone and place the call on the speaker—they were both at Ms. Beatrice house.

"What's up Ashley," Tia asked.

"Where is Keisha?" Ashley asked quickly with fear in her voice.

"I'm on the phone too, what's wrong Ashley?" I asked.

"Alexis just called me cursing, saying that you said the peoples were coming my way and to get everything together and bring it to her crib. Now you know Alexis don't cuss at me, and she didn't use the codes like you told us, so what's going on?" Ashley frantically spit out.

"I don't know baby girl, but we gone find out. I'm gone send Tia to pick you up. Grab a bag and fill it with newspapers. Be ready when she gets there and bring my black duffle bag." The black bag that I was refereeing to was filled with a variety of different guns and heavy ammunition.

"Okay"

"I'm on my way Ashley," Tia advised, before hanging up.

I looked at Tia livid as hell and told her what we were going to do. I told her to get Ashley, while I scoped out Alexis place to see what I could see.

Tia jumped into her car she rented from a fiend, and I drove off in grandmas Buick. I told her to meet me behind the office building. It was one building away from Tia's complex.

***

Meanwhile, things took a turn for the worse for Alexis. The leader of the crew told Marcus and the other one to watch Alexis, while he went to look out for Ashley. The minute he left, Marcus and the other guy went into a corner and started whispering. They came and picked the chair up that Alexis was tied in. Carried her to the bedroom, where they took a wadded up sock and stuffed it into her mouth, then duct taped her mouth to keep it there.

With horror in her eyes, Alexis started to struggle, kick and scream yelling, "No!" Through the sock, but it only came out as a muffled garble. Out of nowhere, a hard blow came to her stomach, taking her breath away and bringing tears to her eyes. It came from Marcus.

"Shut up bitch, don't act like you don't want no dick. I been wanting to hit this pussy," He ripped her blouse open and started to fondle her huge breast.

All Alexis could do was cry and let the two men have their way. Marcus unzipped her pants and pulled them down, while the other guy put the sharp knife to her throat again, saying "bitch just give me a reason." They proceeded to take turns viciously sodomizing her. They forced their massive dicks into her rectum with no lubrication, tearing tissue causing her to bleed on herself. They took turns going from hole to hole at random, laughing and making statements like, "It's good isn't it bitch, this dick you been waiting your whole life for?"

The tears had stopped falling from Alexis' eyes as the pain in her lower region had become numb compared to the pain inflicted upon her heart and mind. Alexis had been praying to God for a miracle to stop this before it happens, a prayer to end it quickly. Soon she begged just to die. The prayers eventually ceased altogether. To Alexis there was nothing. No God, no life, no nothing.

I had been watching the area through a pair of binoculars, from the roof of an apartment building across from Alexis. I could see one of the dumb ass want to be robbers, hiding in the shadows at the end of the building. He had given himself away by the light from the several cigarettes that he smoked. I now knew that this wasn't some police bust, but an attempted jacking.

The question was, where was Alexis? Is she in the apartment? And if she is, who's in there with her?

This dude can't be working this alone, can he?

I doubt that very seriously. Time was being wasted—I called Tia to inform her of the situation at hand. We planned to sneak up on the lookout outside and find out who else was in the house. The problem with that was if we failed, all hell could break loose, and our chances of getting Alexis out would be slim to none. The other plan would be to send Ashley to the door with a bag as intended and get her out of the way before things jumped off, but we had to stay close to the lookout and out of sight.

Ashley drove the car Tia had to the complex. Tia met up with me and we remained in the shadows. We were soon only a few feet away from the lookout, guns ready. Tia was carrying two 9mm's with extra clips, and I was carrying a Tech 9 and two 45 colt commander edition pistols.

As soon as Ashley pulled up and got out of the car, the lookout sprung from his position and ran back into the apartment. As soon as he entered the leader knew that something was wrong. Nobody was in the front room. He quickly made his way towards the back bedroom and could hear the sounds of a muffled cry and grunting. He burst through the door and became instantly infuriated by what he saw. Alexis was lying on her stomach, legs spread wide open, bleeding, as Marcus was about to re-enter her. Before he could, the leader grabbed him by the back of his shirt collar and yanked him to the floor.

"What the fuck are you two dumb mother fuckers doing? We don't have time for this shit! You some sick mother fuckers!"

He picked Marcus up off the floor roughly and shoved him towards the door. "Get your little punk ass to one of the windows and let me know when the little sister make it close to the door. She just pulled up outside. I hope you two dumb motherfuckers didn't fuck this up behind a piece of ass. Because if y'all did, I hope this bitch was worth the shit that I'm going to do to y'all." The leader pulled the other cousin, who had participated with Marcus in the rape, out into the hallway and closed the door—leaving Alexis in the room alone.

Outside, Tia and I quickly ran to Alexis bedroom window as the lookout ran back inside. Staring through the slits of the blinds, we saw and heard the whole confrontation between the leader and the other two men. I sent Tia to stop Ashley. She stopped her at the blind spot where she knew the robbers couldn't see them and sent her back to the car to stall until we came for her. With that done, she made it back to the window where I was. We both could hear the muffled argument between the leader and the other guy, taking place in the hallway. Peeping into Alexis bedroom window, I saw her lying there looking a mess. I tried the window, and it was unlocked. I slowly lifted it up quietly climbed inside, and made my way over to Alexis. When she saw me, she started trying to talk and struggle against her restraints. I shushed her and pointed towards the bedroom door window where Tia was standing, guns aimed. Untying Alexis, I helped her out the window, and made my way out behind her. As soon as we were on the ground, she hugged me and started crying again. I had to shush her. As Tia followed, I motioned for her to get Alexis out of there. She took her to my grandma's car. I hurried to the blind spot and motioned for Ashley to leave. She cranked up the rental and pulled off. Inside of the apartment, Marcus saw Ashley pull off and immediately called out to the others. "Say man—we got a problem. The bitch is leaving!" The two raced from the hallway.

"What?"

The leader yelled as they looked out of the window to see for himself. Ashley was pulling off. "What is that stupid bitch doing? The whispering, knife-wielding rapist asked.

"I don't know," the leader replied, "but go get the sister out here."

With his knife in hand, the cousin hurried to the room and pushed the door open, only to find himself staring down the barrel of my Tech 9.

I told the fool to be quiet by putting my index finger to my lips. While compiling, I forced him to the ground, making him slide his knife towards me. I checked him for other weapons and found a .38 special. Placing my knee on his neck and my gun to his temple, I made him call for the leader. He did this with no hesitation,

"Hey man, come in here for a second!"

As soon as the leader came through the door, I whacked him across the head with my pistol as hard as I could. The unsuspecting blow sent him sprawling to the ground dropping his gun on the carpeted floor. At the same time, Tia was climbing into the window.

Hearing the commotion, Marcus jogged towards the back and entered the room, just as Tia made it through the window and aimed her heat. Laying eyes on Tia and seeing me standing over his two cousins, Marcus took off with incredible speed.

Tia raised her pistol to shoot him, but I stopped her. We didn't need to draw any attention to ourselves. Marcus had run out of the front door into the night, but we'd get him later. With the same strategy and material used on Alexis, we proceeded to bind and duct tape the two. I sent Tia to get the rental from the girls and bring it back here. She made it back quickly but wasn't alone. She had Ashley and Alexis in tow.

"What the hell you bring them for?" I ask.

"Alexis wouldn't let me come back without her," She replied as she was picking up the cold steel blade from the floor.

"What are you going do with these mother fuckers?" Alexis asked heatedly with venom in her voice. She was standing over the two, holding the knife tightly in her hand as if she was contemplating on slitting their throats. From the look in her eyes, the two knew that she would.

I looked at her, all bloodied and bruised, "No the questions is what do you want to do to them?"

She looked at me and then back to them, with a look of murder in her eyes. It had vanished, she smiled and calmly said, "Let me change and get cleaned up." She walked to her closet to find some clothes. "Oh and I don't want Ashley to take any part in this, so let her drive your grandma's car home." We all looked at each other. I could see a change in Alexis.

"Okay," I replied. Then asked, "Are you sure you're up to this shit?" The look that she gave me was enough. I sent Tia with Ashley, to see her off, and had her to back the other car all the way up to the front door. Alexis was dressed and ready to roll. Just as we had finished loading the two wannabe robbers into the trunk. We all hopped into the car and proceeded to drive to a secluded spot in the middle of nowhere, around a place called Riley Lake. Parking the car near the entrance, we all got out and made our way to the trunk. Tia and I unloaded the two by dropping their bodies on the ground. We pulled off their ski masks to see exactly who they were. We had seen them around but didn't know them. But Alexis did. She told us that they were Marcus's cousins.

She didn't know them personally, which is why Marcus' voice was the only one she had recognized back at the house.

Tia and I started in on the two, beating them with our pistols and making them tell us every little detail of their careless robbery. They told us all about how Marcus had come to them and how they had watched us for weeks planning the lick. Alexis stood back, watching their pain in enjoyment until we were through. She stepped forward taking Tia's gun.

"Now it's my turn to deal with you sick mother fuckers," Alexis took the pistol and repeatedly slapped them both across the face with it. She went crazy, beating them over the head, yelling for them to pull their pants down. When neither complied, she continued pounding them repeatedly again.

That's when I grab her in mid swing motion. She stopped.

"Okay, I'm okay. I'm cool—you can let me go," she said calmly. After regaining herself, she went to one and forced the gun into his mouth, sliding it in and out roughly making sure it hit his teeth. Before I knew it, Alexis had pointed the pistol at the leader of the group and squeezed the trigger, blowing off his kneecap. He let out a muffled scream of pure agony trying to reach for the pain with his duct tape hands. The rapist jump after hearing a shot, trying to scuffle backward to get away. Unable to move even if he could, Alexis wasn't having that, she turned to him and struck him across the face with the pistol again. In the evilest voice, I ever heard. Alexis told him, "Bitch ass nigga if you try to move again, I'll blow your fucking brains out." She turn back to the leader, lying on the ground, moaning in pain with blood starting to covering his body.

"You bitch ass nigga! You break into my house and violate my life! Let your boys rape me!" Alexis paced back-and-forth breathing hard and twisting her hair with the hand that wasn't clenching the gun. She stopped in mid step. "Bitch! This shit is your fault," she said firing the gun again. Shooting him in his other leg. She seemed to enjoy his pain as she heard another muffled scream of agony and watched as he tried to reach for his other leg. Alexis stared at him quietly, then suddenly she erupted.

I don't know what was running through Alexis mind at this time, but she was laughing so hard I didn't think she'd stop. Then abruptly, she was serious again. Staring down at the leader in silence, she extended her arm backwards offering the pistol back to Tia. Tia was in a daze for a second until I bumped her in motion with my hand for her to get the pistol. After taking the gun, Tia looked back to where I was standing at me to say "what now." I only gave her a shrug and looked toward Alexis letting her know that it was her call. I wanted her to get it all off her chest. Whatever built up frustration, pain, and rage that was bubbling inside of her. I wanted her to get it out here and now. What she didn't finish I knew we would. We had no choice. Alexis turned her head and attention towards the rapist. She walked over to him, kneeled down beside him, started unbuckling and unzipping his pants. He lay helpless on his back as she pulled his limped dick out and held it in her hand. Alexis began to stroke it and gave him a hand job in the midst of all that was going on. Tia and I looked at each other in confusion as if to say "is this bitch crazy or what?"

Alexis was talking to the rapist seductively. His dick started to rise and harden under her words and touch. "You like that daddy?" she purred, increasing the pace of her stroke. "It's not so bad—it's not so bad. My pussy juice is flowing, and I want you to cum for me daddy, cum for me," she begged, stroking his now full erection.

Confused but lost in the midst of his natural instincts the rapist lay there in pain while trying not to find pleasure in the twisted display but his body over rule is mind. His body became tense, and he came right there lying on his back underneath her steady strokes. She smiled as if she had just satisfied her lover. She asked, "Did you like it, daddy? It wasn't so bad, was it?" she told him soothingly—while keeping the pervert hard by stroking him with her left hand. As the thought of "this bitch done went insane," was running through my mind and I'm sure Tia's. Out of nowhere the gleam of a blade appeared swiftly chopping the rapist penis off in one forceful blow. He screamed in pain so hard the tape gave, and his screams echoed into the sky. He was kicking and screaming as blood shot out, covering him and Alexis. She stood over him laughing uncontrollably as she held his severed member in her hand. Soon the rapist was begging her in pain. Alexis still laughing nonstop, kneeled down with a big smile, stuffing his dick into his mouth. "That was your last nut trick!" You want to rape something? Suck on this bitch! Almost gagging on his own shit. He either passed out from the pain or the loss of blood. The torment of the rapist seemed to satisfy Alexis sick mind as she stood there looking down at him giggling. By this time the leader had gotten one of his foot free and was struggling with pain, trying to get up and get away. I could see things were getting out of control and knew what had to be done. I pulled out the 38 caliber that I had taken from one of them. Pointing it at the leaders head and pull the trigger killing him instantly. Tia followed suit walking over to the rapist who was unconscious and deleted him with one to the head.

We pull their bodies into the lake and let them drift off. The entire time and when we finally got back into the car to leave, Alexis was still giggling. At first at them, and now at herself.

I grabbed her by her shoulders and asked, "Alexis, you gone be alright?" I didn't know what the fuck to think.

"Yes silly. I'm gone be just fine," "she answered.

Something about the way she was acting didn't sit well with me. At the time, none of us knew this, but after all of the trauma that Alexis had just gone through, she would never be that same sensitive, outgoing, warm-hearted person again. Her heart had turned cold, especially towards men.

On our way back to the hood, I thought about the events of the night and thought about how I felt. That didn't take long because I felt nothing. I started going over all of the details in my head, making sure that we didn't forget anything. All weapons were wiped down and thrown into the lake. Except for the one I was carrying that hadn't been used. All blood, tire tracks, and footprints were covered and wiped away with branches, shell casings found and dumped. The only thing out of place was the blood covering Alexis. All we had to do now was get her home and burn the clothes.

The only other problem was that we didn't know how mentally stable Alexis was at this point. These thoughts were brought up because of the constant giggling coming from the backseat. This was wearing on me and Tia last nerves.

"Alexis shut the fuck up with all that giggling! This shit isn't funny!" Tia screamed from behind the wheel of the car, no longer able to ignore the giggles.

This only made Alexis laugh harder, while she was trying to speak. "It…it…is funny Tia. This is the most entertaining night of my life," she said sitting forward in the back seat, hugging Tia while she was driving. "And you helped make it one of the most memorable nights of my life!" she laughed.

Tia was thinking, "This bitch done flipped," as she tried to shrug her off and maintain control of the car. I was in the passenger seat laughing at all of the silliness. We were rolling down the highway, and coming to a stop light in the turning lane heading back to the cities. Alexis was still giggling with her arms wrapped around Tia. As she struggled with Alexis, trying to get her off of her, she eased off the braked pedal, and the car started moving forward. Tia sought to step on the brake and accidentally hit the accelerator, sending the car flying into the middle of the highway.

I immediately grabbed the wheel trying to steer us out of traffic. A vehicle was headed our way, bearing down on us at a fast rate of speed. I hadn't seen it and was trying to avoid the minor traffic and steered directly into its path.

Those were my last thoughts before the eighteen-wheeler slammed head on into the passenger side of the car where I sat.

RETRIBUTION

CHAPTER 7.

Lying in a coma, while Alexis and Tia walked away with only a few broken bones, slight cuts, and bruises. The blood from Alexi's broken nose covered the blood from the crimes we committed earlier. While we were in the hospital Kaylin, accompanied by Rico came to visit us. She was in a state of pain and rage when she saw my condition. Right then, she regretted not taking me back to California. She wanted to know all the details. Tia, feeling obligated and knowing how close Kaylin and I were, told her all the events that had transpired that night. Kaylin was furious but didn't show it.

Meanwhile, as the days passed, the bodies of the two guys were found by some fisherman, on the banks of Riley Lake. Marcus went straight to the police once he heard. He told them about his cousin's intent to rob my crew. He excluded himself from the equation and covered his ass, for not reporting his cousin's intentions saying he didn't think they were serious. Marcus snitching brought the heat down on me, Tia, Alexis, and Ashley.

Even though I was in a coma, I was soon handcuffed to the hospital bed. Tia and Alexis had been released from hospital days earlier, but they all had been detained, being interrogated. That's when Kaylin and Rico stepped into the picture. They hired two of the best lawyers in Minnesota. They had them all quickly released, for lack of evidence. There was still one problem that needed to be taken care of, and that was Marcus. He had been lying low for a few days, but it wasn't long before he came out of hiding. He would be taken care of with a vengeance by Kaylin and Rico.

I was later told that Rico snatched Marcus up one day when he was leaving from the barbershop. They took him to the same secluded spot where his cousin had died. He was found by those same fishermen. The news said his throat was cut from ear to ear and that he was shot in the back of the head several times. If you think Rico did this, you're wrong. It was all by the hands of my sister Kaylin. She had sworn to be there for me and protect me, from the oath taken at our grandma's house before we left for California. And that's what Kaylin did. Refusing to allow Rico to handle what she had sworn to do for the rest of her life. Kaylin felt as if she had failed me. Knowing I was selling drugs, she should've helped, instead of turning a blind eye. Not able to go back and change the past, she sure could get vengeance for my troubles against the person who was the source of those problems. She felt it was all his fault, and that it was her duty to kill him herself.

Entering a new phase in our lives, we've reached a point of no return by adding murder to our resume. I was in a coma for about a good month. If you think everything was all good. You're sadly mistaken—this situation marked me as a major blip on Johnny's law radar.

BREAKDOWN

CHAPTER 8.

After I had came out of my coma, I was arrested on a weapon charge for the pistol I had on me when the car wrecked. They came at me strong and hard with questions about the murders as soon as the doctors cleared me, allowing them to do so.

The officers knew they had nothing on me, except for the weapon charge, but I guess they thought I would crack under pressure. They had nothing to connect me or anybody in the murders except Marcus, who was already dead. Since they couldn't stick me with the murder charges, they charged me with gun possession. They gave me two years in a juvenile detention center. This situation created an intense hatred for my friends and me by Minneapolis finest. These cops would chase me for the rest of my years in the game.

While incarcerated, I spent most of my time educating myself reading everything I could. I finished high school there and became a professor in the school of hard knocks. Because of my quiet demeanor and mature way of thinking, most of the women took me for sensitive. This led to attempts of being bullied. But they were the ones who end up getting fucked. I lost a few battles in the beginning, but I changed after I made it a point to study everyone and everything around me. I taught myself to think on my feet during a fight. If one can harmonize thoughts and actions together, they'll be even more dangerous than the biggest and greatest brawler.

I survive my time locked down and had plenty of love and support from friends and family. The day I was released, before my eighteenth birthday, March 4th, 2003. Kaylin pick me up from the center with the biggest kool-aid smile I have ever seen on her face.

"So what's up little sis?" She asked once we got into the car and pulled off.

"What do you think crazy lady,"

"I think your bad ass is happy to be out and that you're little ass better stay out."

"Well, I'm going to see to that anyway."

"What you want to do first?"

"I want to go see grandma. Do you know if she cooked or not?"

"Now you know that woman cooked you all your favorite dishes." She replied with a grin.

"Well hurry up and get us there. You know I been waiting two years to taste heaven again."

Both of us sharing a laugh as we sped off down the highway while I hung my head out the car window like a dog enjoying the crisp air. It felt good to be free. So good that I could taste it. I didn't know what the future held, but I knew I would tackle it head on and come out on top no matter what.

***

My welcome home party was just right. Ashley, Tia, Alexis, grandma, Kaylin and about 15 to 20 other people from the hood I knew was in attendance. Grandma had cooked all my favorites, the music was bumping, and the vibe was right. Damn, it felt good to be home! I couldn't help but kick back and smile. But as the old saying goes, "a smile turned upside down is nothing but a frown." My smile quickly flipped and turn into that frown at the site of Detective Jay-Jay and Detective Winters also known on the streets as "them peoples."

They pulled up in front of the house sirens screaming and lights blaring as the party was in full swing. They snatched up a little homey who just got out of juvenile detention as well. Someone came and ran to my grandmother. Miss Beatrice, Miss Beatrice the police outside and they messing with Lil Lonnie. "Oh Lord, what these folks want now? My grandmother said as she marched outside to resolve the situation. Grandma walked right to the street where they had Lil Lonnie face down on the hot hood of their cruiser.

"Why y'all bothering these chillens? They ain't doing nothing wrong," she shouted standing on the curb.

"Hello, Miss Beatrice. How are you doing this fine evening? We just thought we would drop by and pay our respects and congratulate Keisha on her new found freedom," Winters reply sarcastically with a big smile. Winters was a tall, overweight white man with the salt-and-pepper hair and bushy eyebrows. Jay-Jay was a tall, slender black man. He used to be a military policeman in the army who had brought the military mentality and style of thinking with him when he came home and joined the force. The Police Department was a perfect fit for him. Jay-Jay and Winters were the hood's worst nightmare. Why? Because they were both crooked as hell and showed no mercy. No, they didn't take bribes unless it was sex from women. Their mentality was just to take whatever they wanted from you. They have power over the streets and who will believe street hustlers versus one of their own.

I had just stepped outside in time to hear the comment about my freedom. "Thank you Detective Winters—you're too kind. Especially since it was you and the Oreo cookie you got with you there that cause me to lose that freedom in the first place." I said with a smile, applauding sarcastically to the detectives.

"You little smart mouth pieces of shit! You think your ass is in the clear from the murders? I swear if that's the last thing I do, I'm going to see your ass fry like the secret kernel recipe before I die!" Winters hollered.

"We're going to get your little murdering ass. You and that little Tia Wagner fucker that runs with you too. And that's a promise if it's the last thing that I do on God's green earth," interrupted Jay-Jay adding to the screaming match.

"Okay detectives, that's enough. Get away from my house and take that profanity with you. This is a house that praises the Lord. Take them devil words away from here. If my grandbaby had killed anybody, she'd be in jail for that. Not home now. So get, for I call somebody to put y'all in your place," my grandma jumped in and said with authority.

"We apologize for the inconvenience Ms. Taylor and

"Keisha we will see your tail soon," Winters said as he pushed Lonnie off the hood of the car. They hopped in and drove off. My grandma came to me with watery eyes and a frown on her face. "Keisha you better get yourself together and get right with God, cause you can see those people don't intend to let you live peacefully. I'm won't always be there to pray for your hard-headed tail, so you got to learn to think for yourself. I see so much of your mother and father in you. I love you baby so please don't break my heart out here trying to get rich. Cash is the root of all evil."

I stood there looking at Kaylin and the rest of my friends as Grandma walked into the house to go to bed. We ended the party early, and everybody went their way. Kaylin stayed home with grandma, and I went to get a room with Michelle. My first night home. Oh, what a night.

***

The next morning I was awakened by the hotel room telephone. I picked it up and put it to my ear. Unprepared for what would come from the other end. Kaylin was screaming historically begging me to get home because something was wrong with grandma. I woke Michelle up and told her we had to go. We made it to grandma's house in recorded time. There was a police squad car and an ambulance parked out front. I jumped out of the car before Michelle could even stop and bolted up the steps into the house. Kaylin was standing in the hallway talking to the police officer when she saw me coming.

"What's wrong Kaylin," I asked, but I was scared to hear the answer.

"I woke up this morning, and the house was quiet, too quiet. You know Grandma wake up early for her coffee and to make breakfast for us. None of that was going on when I got up. I went to check on her, and it looked like she was asleep. Keisha, she was barely breathed." Kaylin was breaking down in tears and hug me while I hugged her back.

"It will be okay, Beatrice Taylor is a fighter, the strongest woman we know." I squeezed her even harder and looked at the officer asking him if I could go back and check on my grandmother.

"Sure I guess, but please let the EMT's do their job," he said. I walked into the room just as EMT's were placing her on the stretcher. "Excuse me could you please tell me what's going on with my grandmother."

"Young lady your grandmother had a heart attack, but she's stable for now. We have to get her to the hospital she's very weak, so if you can excuse us please." the EMT said as he shuffle the stretcher passed me.

My Angel looked so at peace lying there on the stretcher as they wheeled her to the ambulance. I will always cherish that moment of her because that was the last time I saw my favorite girl alive. She died soon after in the hospital. Her heart just couldn't take it anymore. Kaylin and I stayed in the hospital room for what seemed like for hours, holding each other and crying our eyes out. Kaylin kept saying we are all we got baby girl, we are all we got over and over as we rocked in each other's arms.

***

My grandmother's funeral was a surreal event. I still couldn't believe she passed. My rock, my foundation, my world, wasn't there anymore. How could I keep on living without Beatrice Taylor in my corner? All the lessons she had taught me about life, God, and family. All the times my hardheaded tail didn't listen, and all the times I did. My thoughts went to the last time I saw her alive and healthy. The night of my party. Now looking back she looked so weary and tired. I guess she saw another battle on the horizon and just didn't have the will to fight it. But this wasn't her war. This was my war I had brought home. A war that the enemy had brought to my doorstep. A war that I was now ready to fight with all the anger and hurt head on. Anger and pain from the loss of my grandmother. I was entering a new world. The world I plan on conquering whether it be by force or cunning.

JEALOUS TO DEATH

CHAPTER 9.

After the funeral, I took time to contemplate what I wanted to do next. I spent time with the girls when time permitted. Kaylin and I got my grandmother's affairs in order—then we decided it would be best for me to move back to California with her and Rico. This began my rise to the top in the drug game. What did I have to lose? Kaylin was down for the ride and feel just as I did about everything plus it was like she said we all we got.

I put the ladies down on what was about to happen. I would move to California, come back with work, and we would serve the neighborhood up first. Then others would follow until we sewed up the entire city. During that time we would branch out to smaller towns surrounding the city until we owned the whole area. Everybody was down for whatever. We had all formed a bond that couldn't be broken. This was the beginning of hell on earth for Minneapolis, Minnesota.

***

I moved back to California with Kaylin and Rico—we lived on the southwest side of town, life was going as expected. Kaylin and I ran drugs from California to Minnesota, dropping it off with Tia and Alexis. I came back every couple months to check on how things were progressing. The drugs came from Rico and his peoples who was virtually constant supply. We got player prices, so I must admit my rise to the top was relatively easy. It was also because Rico had taken a liking to me. He use to say that I was like his little brother in a woman's body who have gotten killed years ago. I may be a woman, but I have a heart of a street hustler and the desires like a man. He said I was too cool and too smart to have a name like Keisha. I was a woman now.

"Keisha, you go with me every day on runs and have even helped me put some dudes in their places. And through all of that, you never lost your cool or cracked under pressure," Rico told me.

He had never met anyone who was about their money as much as I was at my age. I guess growing up the way we did after my father passed, money was all I thought about. He went on to explain, "I am Ricardo to my friends and family but the streets, they know me as a Rico. You remind me of myself. Not too greedy and not overly ambitious. But at the same time, you're willing to do what needs to be done to get where you need to be and make this paper. And you do these things without blinking an eye. For this I Christian you with the name of Kash."

On this day that street queen was made and will soon grow to epic heights of fame and fortune for a Minnesota chick.

***

I had love for Rico. But his temper and jealousy over Kaylin grew month after month. The more he escalated in the game. He assumed that Kaylin didn't need him anymore and was eventually going to leave him. Knowing this was farther from the truth. During my trips back to Minneapolis, Rico didn't want Kaylin to go along, and I agreed. I told her to focus on finishing school and finding a legitimate job. Which she soon did with a pharmaceuticals company based out of California called Biotech. This corporation would later play a fundamental role in our organization's stronghold on the drug industry.

Kaylin worked in the research and development department. She experimented with all kinds of medicines and chemicals, trying to come up with new and improved drugs. They love Kaylin at Biotech because she was a smart and diligent worker. Rico loved Kaylin whole-heartedly, but at the same time, she was also essential in him maximizing his profit potential off of his drugs. Kaylin took the uncut dope and added just the right amount of cut on it to stretch it. With leaving it at its top quality at the same time. Then there was the fact that she didn't use traditional products to cut the dope. She used a synthetic substance used in medicines that left the high potency of the cocaine intact. For this Rico raked in about an extra thirty percent over his projected profits. So in the end, Kaylin was an asset to maintain. But still, there is an old saying that tells us never to mix business with pleasure or never to let your emotions cloud your judgment. And this was a vital mistake that Rico was about to make.

It seemed with every passing day, Rico's jealousy grew stronger and stronger. It got to the point where Rico would interrogate Kaylin about her whereabouts if she was 10 minutes late coming from work. She couldn't hang out with friends and shopping was done with Rico in tow. This man was virtually smothering her.

Kaylin and Rico would argue but never around me. If there were words to be said and I was around. She would give Rico a look that put him in check and let him know not to make a scene around me. They will then go into the bedroom and argue in hush tones. But they weren't hiding anything from me. I knew what was going on. Just as long as Rico didn't put his hands on my sister, everything was okay.

***

My days were spent with Rico's people and Michelle whenever she got time away from school. I still went to visit Rich's family in the hood from time to time. And occasionally I sent Rich some money and went out to see him when time permitted. He was at a federal prison in California.

I also occupied my time with several correspondence courses, gaining an education in business and psychology. I love to study people and make money so why not master these two subjects.

I also became friends with one of Tia's cousin who had moved from Minnesota to California, but he lived in Compton. Tia's cousin went by the name Jerf. And yes that is the name his mother had given him on his birth certificate.

I liked kicking it with Jerf because he was from home and I could relate to him more than I could with Rico's family. Jerf and his crew were on some flossing and balling type shit. They made money and handled their business. Yet these cats partied extra hard. It was Club Playground or Boulevard every night. I rolled with them occasionally, but it wasn't my type of crowd.

Of course the one night I chose to go out was on one of those nights that my life was to take another dramatic twist. It was about three in the morning when I pulled into the driveway of our house. I could see that Kaylin and Rico's light was still on. As I approached the house, I could hear them arguing. Kaylin had left earlier that night, after getting a call from work informing her that something had gone wrong in the lab on some drugs she was testing. She left about 8 pm and didn't make it back until 1 in the morning. Rico wasn't there when she had left, and she had forgotten her cell phone leaving in such a rush.

When Rico made it home and saw Kaylin wasn't there—naturally he tried to reach her by calling her cell phone, only to hear it loudly ringing up stairs. By the time Kaylin walked through the door, he was drunk and had worked himself into a jealous rage. All hell broke loose. Rico started accusing Kaylin of having an affair and trying to get rid of him.

"That's crazy Rico!" Kaylin cried to the accusations.

"Is it? You act as if we aren't a couple anymore, and I ask you many times to marry me, but you won't set a date!" He screamed.

"You were the one who told me to back away from the game and focus more on my work. My job keeps me busy. Isn't that what your ass wanted? Be careful what you ask. You might just get it!" Kaylin said slamming the door and walking off down the stairs into the den. Rico came after her with rage in his eyes. I was in the kitchen, but neither of them knew that I was home. I listened silently and heard the whole situation starting to escalate.

Staring out of the patio doors in the den, overlooking the pool and back yard. Kaylin was tired. Not just physically, but also mentally of Rico and his jealous tendencies.

"Don't you fucking walk out on me, when I am talking to you woman!"

Rico screamed grabbing Kaylin by the arm, spinning her around to face him. Kaylin could see the anger in his eyes, but he could also see the anger in hers. "Get your fucking hands off me, Rico!" Kaylin said knocking his hands away, then spinning around and opening the glass door that led outside. Then came an unexpected blow to the back of her head that sent her screaming and stumbling out of the door into the patio.

"You bitch!" He yelled after hitting her and stepping out onto the patio. "Who the fuck do you think I am? Don't no bitch talk to me or disrespect me like that!" Rico screamed in a rage. "Your ass is about to learn. I can promise you that!" he said grabbing the backyard water hose from the ground.

He approached Kaylin with it held high as she tried her best to scoot away from him.

I had been listening to them the entire time. Quickly placing my orange juice down and was making my way towards the commotion the minute that I had heard Kaylin scream. Rico nor Kaylin was aware that I was in the house, then Kaylin looked up and saw me coming out of the door behind Rico. Kaylin lifted her leg and kicked him in the nuts.

"Mother fucker!" She screamed, thrusting her foot with all of her might. The blow caused Rico to double over, losing his breath, but also angering him even more. He raised the hose, getting ready to swing the hose at Kaylin until I snatched it from his grip. In one swift motion from behind, I had it held tightly around his neck and was choking him with it. As we struggled, we both became entangled in the water hose.

"Kill his ass, Keisha!" Kaylin screamed. "Kill that mother fucker!"

"I'm going to kill you, Kash," Rico wheezed out as we struggled alongside the pool until we both recently fell in it. I was already short of breath from us tussling, and I couldn't get loose from the water hose that still had us entangled. Holding my breath as we struggled under water, I knew that I was running out of time.

Kaylin saw me struggling to get free. The way the water hose wrapped around his neck and leg, the more he kicked and thrashed, the tighter the water hose became around his neck. Trying to fight for air Rico at the same time squeezing what little air he had left in his body. It wasn't long before his body stopped fighting. He had drowned himself and gave up the ghost.

Kaylin got me free from the hose, and we both swam up to the surface. As I cough, spitting up water, I looked into the pool and say, Rico, still entangled in the hose, floating on his back with his mouth and eyes wide open. My only thoughts were, "Damn, what a fucked up way to die." Something we take for granted every day. A mere breath.

Kaylin was wrapped around me, hugging me tightly, crying and asking me if I was alright. I grabbed her and led her into the house.

"Kash, we killed Rico, his people are gone come after us. They gone want revenge for his death. We just as dead as Rico, Kash."

"I know."

"What we gonna do? What we gonna do?" Kaylin repeated as the tears started flowing and she began pacing back and forth.

"Kaylin stop that shit! And shut the fuckup. So I can think!" Pacing back and forth, Kaylin was wearing on my nerves, but I had to think of a way to get Rico's people off our backs. A way to keep them from killing us, for killing him. The Columbians firmly believes in retaliation and revenge. Not that I was scared to take them out, but their resources and power was unlimited. Rico was affiliated with the Medellín Cartel, the same cartel of leaders such as Carlos Lehder, Pablo Escobar, and Gonzalo Rodriguez Gacha. In fact, Rico was related to Pablo from his father side somewhere down the line.

As I sat there thinking, a plan came together. I explain to my sister what we were going to do. The first thing we did was call the police and ambulance. They arrive to find Kaylin and me soaking wet, and Rico well laid out by the pool. We told him that I had come home from the club and Kaylin was sleeping in her bedroom. On my way to the shower, I glanced out the bathroom window overlooking the pool, and say Rico's body. He was floating in the water tangled in the water hose. I told them. I immediately ran out of the room screaming for Kaylin. She burst out of her room and followed me downstairs to the pool. I dove in and pulled Rico out. I tried to revive him, but it was too late. He was already dead. I also place a bottle of liquor and the glass he been drinking out of earlier on the patio table. The cops bought the entire story. His death was accidental. I placed a call to Rico's cousin Juan and told him about what happened—Rico had gotten himself drunk and somehow tangled up in the water hose, had fallen into the pool and drowned I told him to deliver a Message to Uncle Alejandro. One of the biggest drug distributors in California is also known to be a ruthless and iron fisted businessman.

I had Juan tell Uncle Alejandro not to worry, and I will contact him for a meeting after things have cooled down. I also told him not to let the word out about Rico's death just yet.

The very next morning or should I say later on the day. I got his account book, the keys to his white BMW GS 400 and went to all his spots gathering up all the money he had in the street. His workers know who I was and whom I represented. They also know if they try to play Rico that death was a certainty. I collected two hundred thousand of the two hundred and fifty thousand dollars he had on the streets. That left fifty kilos and one point six million from his stash house. I could have ran with the money. But I would be stupid to play Kaylin and myself like that. It was time for a power move, and I had the perfect plan

PHASE TWO

CHAPTER 10.

Rico's funeral was a week after his death. All of his people were there in full attendance, paying their respects. The services went well. Kaylin sat on the front row with Rico's aunt and cousins. His mother and father had died years ago, and he had no Brothers or sisters left. His aunt Maria was the closest family Ricardo had—she was Juan's mother, Uncle Alejandro's wife.

After the services had been over, Juan approached Kaylin and me.

"I understand that we are all grieving at this, but there is a business to be discussed about the whereabouts of my cousin's assets," he stated.

Kaylin started crying and breaking down on my shoulder, just as we had planned earlier, adding extreme drama to the scene.

"I can't do this right now," she cried.

I comforted my sister and told Juan, "She's still too broken up over Rico's death. I know that you want to discuss business. And I say this with the most honesty respect towards you. I don't feel comfortable talking to you about this situation. And Rico told me that if anything happened,

Uncle Alejandro would take care of everything. So I asked to speak with your father to discuss this matter. He is the only one I feel comfortable talking to."

I could see the Juan didn't approve of my request. That moment Juan started to hate me for my gesture. He thought that I had an ulterior motive because there was a significant amount of money at stake.

Juan went over to his father and told him of Kaylin's fragile state of mind and my request. He told Juan that now was not the time to discuss business and to have me meet them at the restaurant in Hollywood.

***

I arrive at the restaurant later that night, riding in Rico's BMW. Walking through the back doors, I was escorted to the private office where Uncle Alejandro ran his empire. He was seated in his moderately decorated suite smoking a Cuban cigar. I nodded to the big solid built man who had survived many drug wars. He motioned for me to take a seat in one of the chairs across from his desk. Juan stood in the corner leaning against the file cabinet viewing me with an eye of suspicion.

"So Kash here we are," Alejandro said in his thick Hispanic accent. "My nephew spoke great things about you. He told me you and your beautiful sister were like one of us. He would trust you two with his life. Now I ask you is that true?"

"Yes, it is Uncle Alejandro. Rico was the brother I never had."

"And he to look upon you as a sister," he told me as if reminiscing. Then added, "it's unfortunate the way he died. I love that young man as if he were my son."

Lowering my head, feigning remorse and tears, I said. "I tried to save him, but it was too late. I'm sorry Uncle Alejandro."

"No, no, no. You did what any person would do. Now tell me, what do you have for me? My nephew owed me a considerable amount of assets, and I was told that you have been playing collector."

"I was only looking out for the family's best interest."

"Well good then, what do you have for the family?" he asks with a big smile.

I dug into my pocket and put out the keys to Rico BMW and toss them into the desk. Uncle Alejandro picked them up with his fingers and held them up letting the BMW logo on the key chain spin back-and-forth. He then asks, "What is this?"

"The keys to his car," I stated a matter of fact. Juan angrily pushes himself off the cabinet and rushed over to me with his finger in my face.

"This is not a game. Rico owed us a lot more than a damn car!"

"Juan, sit down!" Alejandro said forcefully then continued. "Leave the girl alone. He did not owe us anything—he owed me. Do you not know whose presence you're in? Must I remind you day in and day out that even though I love you my son. I will not tolerate disrespect." he warned.

"Now Kash, do you understand what's going on here?"

"Yes sir, I do"

"Well, then you know that I was talking about more than just an automobile?"

"Yes, I do. Inside of the trunk of the car is two hundred thousand dollars of the two hundred and fifty thousand he had out on the streets. That other fifty will come in as soon as the brokers pay up. There are fifty kilos and one point six million in cash that came from his stash house. I figured you wouldn't want to be bothered with the small things. My sister and I knew what was being required of us and act accordingly. The only reason Kaylin isn't here is that of the grief of her losing Rico. She loved him. I love him, and we're both going to miss him. I know you didn't know about the savings. Kaylin and I don't feel entitled to it since Kaylin and Rico weren't married yet. So I present it all to you, his family."

When Uncle Alejandro heard all this, he was visibly shocked. An average person would have taken the small fortune and ran. Alejandro gave the keys to Juan and told him to park the car in the private garage of an apartment complex where a big portion of drugs was stored. He then turns his focus back towards me.

"Now Kash back to you. This is the most honorable thing that you have done. You and your sister honestly won't be unnoticed. The house that you and your sister live in is already in her name, so you will keep the house for yourself."

"Thank you."

"Wait I'm not finished. I'm also giving your sister six hundred thousand dollars. That should be enough for her to get along with her life. I would also ask that your sister consider staying on and working for us. Her abilities are much needed in our organization."

"I'll speak to her about it,"

"Good, good. Now tell me, my young friend, what can I do for you?"

I didn't answer right away. I was acting hesitant, given the I impression that I was afraid to ask.

"Tell me my friend don't bite the tongue. Anything you ask of me is yours. My nephew loves you and your sister, and I loved him so tell me."

"Well, I thought maybe I could invest with you. I have money of my own. I've been hustling over the past couple of years, and my thing in Minnesota is pretty profitable. I just lack a major connection such as yourself."

"Yes, yes, say no more. My nephew has mentioned your situation a time or two. But your money is no good to me, and if you do this, I must know that you can handle the business."

"I know I can."

"If I do this thing for you, I don't want you going out there half stepping. You will be representing me, Alejandro Moreno. Any problems that you have, I will have. Understood?"

"Yes,"

"Good, now let me think," He said rubbing his chin.

"This is what I give you. First, the car is yours and the stash house with all his belongings. I'll start you off with twenty of the fifty kilos, and the fifty thousand that is still on the streets belongs to you. Is this satisfactory my friend."

"Yes Uncle Alejandro, it is more than satisfactory."

"Just honor your word with me, and I will honor mine with you." We both stood and shook hands. He told me to join him for a late dinner in the restaurant, while we waited for Juan to bring the car back with Kaylin's and my portion.

***

It seems as though our future was starting to look a little brighter. Kaylin and I were practically millionaires overnight. But our good fortune was about to shine even brighter. This move would be the necessary boost that I needed to take my crew to the next level. I have the backing of a major figure on the drug scene, initiative and drive to accomplish my goal.

Uncle Alejandro respected me for my gesture and thought that I was a woman of honor who could be trusted. Many kingpins wouldn't work with women in the drug game. But again I'm not your average female. But what he didn't know was that all I was doing was playing my psychological games on him. To maneuver him into a position where I needed him to be. Why take the money and run, when I could make him give it to me? I bet you're asking, "but he didn't give you all the money and product?" No, he didn't, but eventually he will. Eventually, he'll give me that and much more. I'm not a compulsive greedy woman. Those are the fools that play themselves by being blinded by greed. I use patients as a deterrent to foolishness and look at the bigger picture. Greedy by nature but I've learned to tame my greed. Alejandro allowed Kaylin and I some down time to mourn

Rico before I got to work. Plus, he wanted to set up his mules that he would use to transport the work from California to Minnesota.

We decided that it was time to moved back to Minnesota. Two years had passed since I had moved to California. Kaylin had a job to think about which wasn't all that important now that she had the six hundred thousand from Rico's uncle and our savings. Kaylin told her job that she was taking a definite amount of time away from her job, to get over the grief of losing her fiancé. She held a high position within the company, so they were ok with her leaving knowing she would come back. We told Alejandro that it was too painful for Kaylin to be in the house. It always reminded her of Rico and the love that they once shared. So finally Kaylin and I were going back to Minnesota. The day before Kaylin and I were to leave. We were at the house packing our belongings, waiting for the movers when there was a knock at the door.

"Damn who is that this late in the day?" Kaylin asks, getting up from packing a box on the floor to answer the door. When she opened it there was a skinny white man dressed in an expensive suit.

"Excuse me. I'm looking for Miss Kaylin" he stated.

"Yes, that's me."

Kaylin Jefferson? He asked again but this time stating her full name.

"Yes, I am she, but whom may I asked are you sir?

The man extended his hand with a big smile to accompany it, he said. "Oh, I'm sorry, excuse my manners. My name is Robert Clark. I work for Amica Trust and Insurance. I'm sorry, but I had to make sure that I had the right person. May I come in Miss Jefferson to sit and have a word with you about a business matter."

"I apologize to you now Mr. Clark for my manners. Yes, you may come in." With a sincere smile, Kaylin opened the door wide enough to show him that he was welcome. Mr. Clark came into the living room where I was amongst all of the boxes. Mr. Clark, this is my sister, Keisha, introducing me. Mr. Clark reached out, and I stood to shake his hand.

"Please excuse the mess—we are in the middle of packing."

"Miss Taylor, I don't mean to pry, but may I ask why you're moving away from such a beautiful home."

"Well, my fiancé just recently passed. He accidentally drowned in our pool out back. Staying here is too painful. It draws too many memories," Kaylin said with a hint of sadness.

"Oh, I see. What a terrible thing, but Mr. Pérez wouldn't want you to grieve over him. He would want you to move on with your life." Clark stated.

This stunned Kaylin and I both, I was compelled to ask. "Mr. Clark, you knew Ricardo?"

"No Ms. Jefferson, I didn't know him, know him, but I knew him. He is the reason that I am here. Mr. Pérez loved you very much. He used to tell me these things during our meetings. He wanted to make sure you were taken care of and able to continue, in the case of his untimely death. All good reasons for him to take out a life insurance policy. The policy pays out exactly One million dollars to you Ms. Jefferson.

"Oh my God," was all Kaylin could manage to say, covering her mouth.

"Wait, Ms. Jefferson, there is more. There was also what we call a double indemnity Clause, which in the event of accidental death, as the autopsy report has determined, the policy pays double."

Kaylin and I both stood speechless staring at him in shock.

"So, Ms. Jefferson," he continued. "I am here to present you with a check for 2 million dollars and a key to a safety deposit box that Mr. Pérez wanted you to have. I hope that these things will be enough to help you overcome your grief."

Sitting there with our mouth wide open and jaws hanging to the floor, Kaylin and, myself for that matter, was blown away by the news. We couldn't move. We were shocked beyond belief. Kaylin sat there in an almost catatonic state until Clark asked. "Ms. Jefferson, Uh… are you alright?"

"Yes, I'm all right," Kaylin answered, finding her voice.

"Well, that's good, because I have some papers here for you to sign and I need to see some identification to verify who you are. No offense, it's just procedure."

"None was taken, Mr. Clark."

Mr. Clark pulled out the necessary papers and let Kaylin signed them. After the process was completed, he shook her hand and told her that if she ever needed anything in the area of banking. He was the man to call.

"Ms. Jefferson, I knew Mr. Pérez very well on the business front. I handled things over, and under the table also," Clark stated winking his eye and smiling as he walked out of the door heading to his car.

When Mr. Clark was gone, Kaylin and I both looked at each other smile and started jumping for joy hugging each other and screaming.

"Keisha, what are we going to do with all this money?"

"I don't know. I was thinking about that while you were talking to Mr. Clark."

"And what did that big old brain in that big old head come up with?"

"Sis, you know how you were saying that the only reason Biotech gave you this indefinite leave of absence was because they needed you."

"Yeah."

"And you said that you could do all of the research and stuff on your own if you had your research lab and research team?"

"Yeah"

"Would it be hard for you to get something like that started? And how much would a place like that cost to get off the ground?"

"With the experience and expertise, I'm pretty sure I could get FDA approval to open up my own research lab. Not only that, I could probably get support and funding from my job, if I gave them exclusive rights to any new product of their choosing. And Keisha you know that you and I both already own shares of stock at my job, so that'll be a big plus but why not just invest more?"

"Because Kaylin, if you do that they'll control our interest and have creative control over your work. But with your own research lab, you're in control, and you won't have anyone looking over your shoulder. Plus you could open the lab any place you want. Now, how much do you think it'll take to get his thing off the ground?"

"You know Keisha. You just might be onto something here? Minneapolis will fight for the opportunity to have a new company like that open up there. As you know, it will be under the title as a subsidiary of Biotech. Having my job name associated with their city will be too big of an opportunity to pass up. If we promise to employ local people to help out with their job market. I'm thinking that my company would match our funds dollar for dollar. It would take somewhere in the ballpark figure of ten million to get us started and we could get a loan."

"Well, we're definitely going to need some help with this. I'll call Michelle in the morning, and I want you to get on the phone with your job and the banks. It also may be wise to call Mr. Clark to see what kind of help he's willing to offer. Let's put this move on hold until we can get things in order."

All right, but won't this investment drain us of all our new found fortune? And you know as well as I am aware that it'll take a while before this company could turn a profit."

"Yeah, I know, we're going to build an empire here, and drug money alone ain't going to get it. We both need to just sleep on it and see what tomorrow brings. Now get some rest girl. Oh, and Kaylin, always know that I got your back and that I love you."

"I love you too Keisha," she said kissing me on the cheek, giving me a big hug and heading upstairs to bed.

The next day Kaylin and I went to work, seeing if we could recruit the necessary help we needed to get this business venture going. Kaylin called several banks but was given minimum loan figures. She called her job. After ten different phone calls, and going up the chains of command. She was finally able to get a hold of the vice President of the company. He promised to talk to the board at their morning meeting and get back to her. She also called Mr. Clark who was more than thrilled to help out for five percent of our profits. He got the necessary bank on board. The loan would be for three million if we match it and promised to do all of our banking through them. I contacted Michelle and brought her up to speed on what we were trying to do. She lent her accountant expertise, providing us with several loopholes to get the money rolling. By the end of the day, everything was set into motion except for us waiting to hear from Biotech. Then they finally call that afternoon around four-thirty, which was for a meeting in two days. They wanted a full business plan and a representative from the bank to attend the meeting. We spoke with Mr. Clark, and he agreed to have some of his best people over to help us get it all together so we can seal the deal. He has given us the full resources of Amica Trust and Insurance. After this, I called Michelle in to help us out. She had just received her bachelor's degree and was gearing up to go back in for her masters.

Over the next two days, we got the presentation together and Kaylin vigorously rehearsal and studied the ins and outs of the computer graphics slide sheets. Michelle drilled her on the figures, did a projection of the profit potential's, and then prepared her for any questions that Biotech might come with.

The meeting was held at Biotech corporate office. On our side of the table were Kaylin, Mr. Clark and Michelle representing our team. I waited outside patiently in the lobby while things are being discussed. An hour and a half later, Kaylin, Mr. Clark, and Michelle came out with smiles on their faces. Everything went well. Kaylin and Michelle had to explain that Biotech wanted to loan a comparable figure six point five million to gain a controlling interest in the company. But Mr. Clark is a brilliant and resourceful man— he cut them off at the pass. We would only let them invest five point nine million, with a phased buy-out plan on our end. With this, we would give them back three million with interest, and for our benefit, their presence would be felt less.

All was well, but I had one more call that needed to be made. I had to call Uncle Alejandro to put my side plan into place. The side plan was to purchase two hundred kilos from him at nine thousand a piece totaling one point eight million. After Kaylin put her cut on it, I was able to turn the two hundred into two hundred and sixty kilos. We would drop them wholesale back in Minnesota for eighteen thousand a piece, turning a profit of a little over three million dollars. That would provide us with enough to go into business with Biotech and leave us with a little over two million dollars to work with in the game.

I met with Alejandro, and he agreed to the deal and reminded me that I still owed him for the twenty I had got earlier from him

A WORD FROM THE WISE

CHAPTER 11.

I hadn't talked to Tia since the day before Rico's burial. She didn't know what was going on and I needed to get her and the team ready for what lay ahead. The team had to line workers up and set the stage for this flood of drugs that were about to come their way. I dialed her number and Tia picked up after the first ring.

"What's up Kash?"

"You,"

"I can't see. I ain't heard from you in about a month. I thought them Columbia mother fuckers might've cut your throat and stuck you in a box .

"Naw, you know your girl got a gift for gab and can talk a tiger out his striped if need be."

"I hear you playa, but on the real. The snow is melting down my way, and it's about to dry all the way up."

"Don't trip—your girl got you. But I need you to answer one question before I go on."

"Yeah what's that?"

"Are you ready to be rich and ball beyond your wildest dreams?"

"First off, that's two questions. And to answer both, yes. So what you got for me?"

"Well, we'll talk about that when I get there tomorrow. Get the girls together, and we'll meet at The W. Bring your game face because this is the realist shit you about to encounter."

"I keep my game face on baby. You make this sound like we are about to hit the lottery."

"The lottery ain't got shit on what we about to do. It's time to take over."

"All right, I'll holler at you then."

"Okay." I sat back on the couch contemplating all that I had on my plate. This was a high-stakes game of chess, and one wrong move could fuck everything up. I have to play it close because this is for me and mine. There isn't anything or nobody that's going to get in our way. I put that on Beatrice Taylor. I got up to finish packing my bag and to get ready for my flight in the morning.

***

The very next morning, I arrived in Minnesota. After leaving budget car rental. I checked into the suite that I had reserved at The W, took a shower and then hit the pavement on a mission to get things ready for this meeting. I have special things planned for today, and I couldn't wait to see my crew.

Later in the day when everyone arrived at the hotel room, I had an immaculate dinner set with fine China, and wine glasses greeted them.

"Damn Keisha, oh, I mean Kash," Alexis exclaimed at the sight before her, then corrected herself.

"Yeah, big Sis, what's all this?" Ashley ask.

"Damn bitch what's the special occasion?" Tia questioned.

"Well my friends, the occasion is us," I stated.

"Hey, I can get with this shit," Ashley teased.

"I'm sure you can Ashley, but it's more than that. We are about to take over the city. We've come into a substantial amount of money. And these funds have already been turned into drugs." I told them holding up my hands to stop that onslaught of questions about to come at me from them. "but first," I added. "Let us eat and drink. Then we'll get down to the business. Plus I have a few gifts for my loved ones. I also want you to contemplate on what I'm about to drop on you all."

We sat at the table, eating steak and lobster and drank wine. We laughed, joked and had fun. There was a lot to celebrate. Me being home again. I loved these three as much as I love Kaylin. Watching all of them, wondering if either of them had any idea what was about to come either way. I glanced over at Alexis. After her assault she found her escape through relationships with other women. She was a beautiful rose and loyal. These are the people that I would put my life on the line for. This was my family.

After dinner was over with, we all sat in the living room section of the suite, sipping our drinks and smoking a blunt that Tia had just rolled up. I could see the looks of impatience and anticipation written upon their faces. They all wanted to know just what I had up my sleeve. I've been recognized for my surprises in the past, and I didn't aim to disappoint this time. Tia, as usual, was the one trying to get it out of me finally.

"So Kash, talk to me baby. What's all the talk about?"

I smiled, took a sip from my drink, and leaned back in the oversized chair that I was sitting in. All eyes were on me.

"Well, it's like this. I feel we've been half stepping."

"What the fuck you talking about Kash? We have been doing all we can."

"Shit, we one of the top dope dealing bitches. We getting money on top of money!" Tia answered defensively.

"Yeah, Kash. You know we be out in these streets putting in work and riding for the cause," Alexis added.

"I didn't say y'all be half stepping. I said we! It's time for us to power up to a whole new level. Yeah, we getting money, but nothing like what's coming. A lick bigger than either of us has ever seen."

"Now, this is the business. We have to get rid of two hundred and sixty kilos, and we have to do it immediately."

Everybody's jaws dropped when I said this. They couldn't believe it. We had gone from slanging a few keys to working a few hundred.

"Dawg, who you killed?" Tia asked in a joking but serious tone.

"Well, since you all are my family, and there are no secrets between us. I will lay it all out in the open. It all started one night when I came home from the club kicking it with your cousin Jerf…"

I sat there for about an hour, explaining to them what happened that night with Rico. My meeting with Uncle Alejandro, the life insurance policy, and the help from Michelle and Mr. Clark. I even told them how we had to flip this money and get it back to Kaylin. So we could get our legal business with Biotech off the ground. I also told them about how I had gotten a platinum visa card from Mr. Clark before I left Cali, on Kaylin's account.

"Now let's take this credit card and do a little shopping before the package gets here. We need to get the trap houses and stash houses together. But before we do that, I have one more thing for you Tia," I exclaimed with a smile. "You been my sister for years. I can never repay you for your friendship. But this is a small token of my appreciation." I reached into my pocket and fished out the keys to Rico's car and handed them to Tia.

"Here, these are the keys to that BMW outside. The one I got from Rico. It's all yours."

"Bitch, you giving me a dead man's car? The man you killed?" Tia stepped to me, took the keys and gave me a big hug and kissed me on my cheek. "Thanks, girl, I love you too," she laughed.

You see there was significance behind that car. It was like a trophy. A prize for the work that I had put in and I was passing this award to Tia and no one ever part from their trophy.

We went throughout the day securing rental property through Alexis and Ashley's mother small realty company. After that, we shopped at Home Depot and Best Buy. Then hit the block and gathered up a few cheap laborers to install the reinforced doors, bars, cameras, and other stuff onto the houses. They were impenetrable. Next, everyone sat out to gather their crews to work the territories assigned to them.

Alexis was given Saint Paul, Wisconsin, and Chicago. She used a team of ladies that took care of her business. Although they were women, after seeing them in action, people knew they weren't to be underestimated. They could and would get just as down and dirty as any man.

Ashley was assigned to the North Side and all suburban areas surrounding. Her clique was made up of her male cousins, so she just called the shots. Because Tia was always lurking in the shadows, there weren't many problems we came across.

The biggest territory was South Side of Minneapolis, and occasionally Arizona. I had let Tia take because of her higher street knowledge of Minneapolis. The South was always beefing with other sides, but Tia kept it business all the way around and didn't get involved in the petty beef between the hoods. The real beef she had to deal with was the East side of Saint Paul and Selby block. Simple minded folks that tried too hard. Ashley's territory, putting the fear of God into her cousins.

I was left with California where we originally were based. I thought it would be better that I worked common grounds. These were our territories, and we bled the streets with a vengeance when we first got started.

The Chevy Impala's that were ordered came within a week. These were our mobile control centers installed with stash boxes and police scanners. Where and how we kept an eye on everything and everyone. Alexis and Ashley had an uncle that was a high-ranking officer in the Minneapolis police department, and his son was in the police academy. Their uncle wanted to be the thug that wanted to get paid, so he kept us with current scanner codes. Even the ones for the Narcotics team. His thought it was an ambitious hobby to sit up and listen to various police bands. He went out his way to help us.

Everything was set up and had been running smoothly. Until one Sunday afternoon when I pulled up on 38th and Chicago to the Cubs Foods corner store on the south side. Driving my Yukon. I jumped out and greeted everyone who was standing around like I usually do. As I was on my way into the store, an elderly lady was on her way out. She stopped as soon as she passed me and said, "Keisha?"

I stopped and looked around to see who it was. It was Ms. Maggie Jones, one of my Grandmothers good friends.

"Baby, come over here and give Aunt Maggie a hug. I haven't seen you since your grandma died. But I been praying for you. You and your sister. Matter of fact. The Lord has been dealing with me about you lately. He keeps pressing on my heart to let you know to stop playing patty cake with the devil before he leads you out of his protective circle. Now I don't know what you doing girl. I don't rightly care, but if it isn't according to the word of God. You better stop it and get your tail back on the right path because God don't like ugly."

"Good lord!" was all I could think to myself when Aunt Maggie starting talking. This woman's mouth ran a mile a minute. I often wondered where she found time to breathe. She was jabbering on about the Lord and how he was using her. I'm thinking to myself, "Yep! She's had a few too many glasses of wine at communion and has finally fallen off her rocker."

"Now Keisha I'm not going to preach to you, but I got to let you know that the Lord talks to all of us. We just don't hear him most of the time because we ain't in tune with the Spirit. You see, God has us traveling on his road of life and on this road He gives us signs. Half of us don't follow those signs. We just want to travel that path the best way we think we should. But what happens when you're lost on the road?" Aunt Maggie paused for a second, then continued before I even had a chance to answer.

"I'll tell you what happens. He puts out another sign for you to see, so you can find your way back to the right path. And Keisha, this right here is one of those signs young girl. Mark my words, one day you're going look back on this day and know that this was a sign." She had an intense look on her face as she held my stare with a seriousness in her eyes as I had never seen before. It was as if she was literally trying to drill her prophetic words into my brain. Then in the blink of an eye, she broke into a huge smile. With joy in her eyes, she asked, "Now how's your sister doing? I ain't seen that child since your grandma's funeral." She then went on and on without allowing me to answer her many questions. We stood there talking for the better part of thirty minutes or so. She ended with an invitation to come and attend church with her at our old church house. The one we use to attend with our grandma faithfully.

During my drive, I thought about all that Aunt Maggie had to say. I wondered if what she was telling me was a sign from God. Was it a sign from my grandma? I didn't know, but it felt good talking to her. Mainly because it brought back feelings of grandma. I felt like I was really back at home again. My mind went back to wondering if grandma was talking to me through Aunt Maggie. Naw, it was just the fact that they have been around each other for so many years that the words coming out of her mouth just sounding like grandma.

Shaking off Aunt Maggie words. I came back to reality and put my mind back on the business that needed to be handled. I wanted no parts of the spiritual world right now. If anything, running into her reinforced my drive to succeed in my business dealing to prove that my grandmother was right. The moment that thought passed through my mind—flashing blue lights and the sound of sirens interrupted it. I peeped into the rearview and could see the two assholes that were pulling me over. It was Jay-Jay and Winters.

ONE ON ONE

CHAPTER 12.

I pulled over to the side of the road and parked the truck. Remaining inside, I watched as the two of them eased up the side of my whip, one on the passenger's side, and the other on the driver's side. Winters knocked on my driver's side window and asked me to roll it down. He had a great big smile on his face like he had just scratched off a million dollar lottery ticket. I let the window down.

"Well, well, well. If it ain't our friend Keisha Jefferson, aka Kash. All dolled up in her brand spanking new Range Rover. I wonder what poor sucker you killed to get this baby," he said as if he were talking more to Jay -Jay instead of me.

"You know the routine little girl, cut the engine off and step out of the vehicle," he added with more authority in his tone.

I complied and cut the engine. Then opened the door and stepped out. As soon as my feet touched the pavement, Winters spun me around towards the truck and pushed me up against it. He then kicked the inside of my ankles, showing that he wanted me to spread them.

"May I ask what the problem is officer?"

"Shut your trap you little piece of shit," Jay-Jay said joining in.

"You got any drugs or weapons on you?" Winters asked as he patted me down.

"No," I replied.

"What you got in the truck?" Jay-Jay asked glaring inside.

"Nothing sir. I'm a piece of shit remember. Therefore pieces of shit can't possess anything. At least that's what the real world seems to think. So I guess you and your friend here got to go back to la la land and go fuck yourselves," I stated with a smile.

"Did you hear what this little mother fucker just said Winters? I ought to put a hot one in your little smart ass mouth," Jay-Jay spat back.

"Whoa, Whoa partner, cool your heels. You see all this little bastard is doing is trying to get a rise out of you. But she doesn't know that we know her, and her little drug dealing ass crew are the major hitters out here on these streets. How do you think we knew to pull your truck over? It's only a matter of time before we nail your drug dealing, murdering ass to a wall." Winters stated added emphasis to his last words.

"You two pigs some dirty mother fuckers, I said shaking my head. Before I knew it, Jay-Jay caught me with a small blow to the stomach that felt like I was hit with a sledgehammer. I doubled over and the second officer kicked me to the ground and then kicked dirt and dust in my face. Walking away, Winters looked down and said, now look at who's the dirty mother fucker." They then laughed walking to their patrol car and driving off. Leaving me lying beside my truck in the dirt. I decided that the two mother fuckers had to be dealt with. I already blamed them for my grandmother's heart attack.

Getting up off the ground, I thought of my grandma again. The things that Aunt Addie Mae had mentioned. At the end of my thoughts, I came to the same conclusion. I had business to handle. The events of the day only added to my reinforcement to prove that my grandmother was right. That was special and to get as rich as I could. Reach the point where I was untouchable. And being untouchable was what I needed to be. That I was getting ready to kill two cops, this shit just got real.

When Kaylin had arrived back to Minnesota, she had leased us a house out in Blaine. She got it in an exclusive upper class mixed neighborhood. She handled getting the house together while I managed the street business. After the run in with the police, I called a meeting over to the house. I informed them of the events that took place, not including my run in with Aunt Maggie. I told them all about the crooked ass cops and how they could be a problem. "They could jeopardize everything we're trying to do here."

"I told you how the motherfuckers were when you were living in California," Tia said.

"I heard you then, and I hear you now Tia. We got too much on the line this time to let them bitches get in our way" I blast back.

"But what can we do Kash? They the police," Ashley wanted to know.

"We get rid of them dirty motherfuckers Ashley," I stated.

"Now that's what I'm talking about. Kill these punk pussy police ass bitches. I'm sick of they assess fucking with us anyway." Alexis jumped up hollering at the prospect of killing those crooked cops.

"Whoa, whoa, whoa Kash that's a drastic step. Plus it's gone bring a lot of heat down in the streets. And with that much heat on the streets, how we gone hustle?"

"If anything, this move would only slow progress down," Kaylin pleaded being the voice of reason.

"Yeah girl your ass in Minneapolis Minnesota. These hoes ain't about to let your black ass kill one of their own and get away with it. No sir bob," Tia added her two cents in with her usual touch of humor. Suddenly everybody tried to talk all at once. The room was filled with a bunch of gibberish.

I held up my hand and protest and told everybody to listen. "I didn't say that we were going to kill them. Well, not just yet. If it comes to that, it will be the last resort, and we could call Uncle Alejandro in for that and let his people handle it. No sense in getting her hands dirty, better to use out of town talent. What I was suggesting was that we set them dirty bitches up. You know they like to get paid, and they love pussy. So we get the bitches on tape, send it to the feds and get them off our back. Simple as that."

Tia was the first to speak raising her hand as if we were all in the classroom. "You my girl and I love you to death, but I want to know one thing."

"What is it, Tia?" I asked bracing myself for sarcasm.

"Man is you crazy? What the hell have you been smoking? Give me some of that shit," she said, and everyone burst out into laughter. When everyone calmed down, I asked if they thought it could be done. Ashley was the first to speak this time.

"Yes, I think it can be done. I got this home girl whose brother was wanted for questioning in a drive- by a few months ago and those same police officers came over looking for him. She said at that fat nasty Winters try to get is holla on. But she says she couldn't see it. He likes chubby dark skinned broads.

"I think you might be onto something."

"So what do you think Kaylin?" I asked my big sis.

"Just know what your ass is doing Kash."

"Tia?"

"Shit sounds crazy. I say stay the fuck out of the pit that's filled with vipers. But no, you're hungry ass want to jump into a pit of hungry vipers with the fat white mouse in your hand. Yeah, I'm down, but I still think this shit is crazy."

"And you Alexis? "I asked.

"Kash you are my rock. Whatever you think is right you know I will back you up."

And with that, we agreed to put a plan into motion to set up them crooked ass police officers and get them out of our hair.

***

Afterward, Tia dropped Ashley off at home and then headed home herself. Kaylin went to the movies to catch this romantic comedy she been dying to see. That left Alexis and me alone. While I was cleaning off the coffee table. Alexis looked at me and said, "Kash I know you like to keep most of your feelings bottled up. But I can tell by the way you were talking earlier that this whole run in with the officers bothered the hell out of you. We were dealing with them fools for the past couple of years while you were in California. I know they can be a pain in the ass, but I want you to know if you need to talk to somebody I'm here for you."

I looked at her and listened to the sincerity in her voice. It was touching, the love she had for me. I hesitated for a moment—then spoke. Alexis cut me off.

"Kash, you're more than my employer. You're the only woman that I've ever loved. If it wasn't for you Kash, I probably would had killed myself a long time ago. You save me on that fucked up night, and for that, I'm forever grateful. My son is forever thankful that you save his mother's life. And for those reasons Kash, my life is indebted it to you. This bitch right here, will ride or die for the ones she loves. You're one of the people I love the most, and it hurts me to see something bothering you. I would like to help if I can please trust me and let me assist you like you helped me in the past."

She jumped up and wrapped her arms around me, embracing me with her love. Alexis had her head buried in my chest with her arms wrapped around my waist. I could feel the wetness of her tears soaking through my shirt. Her tears and sniffles made my heart surrendered. I pulled back from her, put my index finger under her chin and raised her head so I could look into her eyes. The tears flow for those big beautiful puppy dog eyes. All I can do was smile at her.

I said "Alexis you're not the bitch that rider or dies for me—you're the woman that I know love me enough to travel to the ends of the earth and back." I wiped the tears from her eyes. She's smiled at me and rubbed her cheek against my hand, then kissed it. She looks at me as our faces move closer to one another. Our lips met, and we kiss each other. It seems as if the time had stopped, and the world as we knew it cease to exist around us. By the time we separated, we were both out of breath.

Alexis grabs my hand and leads me to my bedroom. We both started to undress each other. When I had her down to her panties and bra, I ask

"Are you sure you want to do this?"

She only smiled at me. Placed a gentle kiss on my lips and said in almost a whisper "why wouldn't I want to be with the only woman I ever loved."

She continued to strip me out of my clothes, and I slipped her out of the rest of hers. I had forgotten how beautifully sculpted, and soft her body was. Her curves symbolizing the power of her womanhood. The heat of her body just as hot as the moisture between my legs. She pushed me down on the bed and ran our hands over my body as she knelt in front of me. She kissed me from my neck to my nipples then making her way down my stomach. I laid on the bed lost in the passion and love that Alexis and I were sharing. She stuck one finger, then two inside my wet walls. I sat up motioning for her to meet me as we kissed deeply. Tears began to spill from her eyes. Seeing the look in my eyes, she told me everything was fine. She knew I kept my toys in my top drawer next to the bed. Without breaking our kiss, Alexis reached over and grabbed my strap on. The second we broke for air I pulled the strap-on up on me. Crawling on top of me, Alexis spread her thighs across my body and straddled me. I watched her shuddered as she slowing eased her body down allowing my brown rubber dick to enter inside of her. She began working her hips. The love making session lasted for hours as we pleased each other. Afterwards, we lay and embraced in each other's arms, cherishing the moment in our minds. The heat of our bodies hot to the touch only cooling as our temperatures descended from its peak. We were both drained and highly appeased.

As I held Alexis, my thoughts soon drifted to the past. After the traumatic events of the night she was raped, she had been repulsed by the touch of a man. She had made up in her mind that she will never give herself to a man again in that way.

Seeing my expression and knowing me almost better than Kaylin, Alexis knew that I was in deep thought. She looked over at me, place a soft hand on my cheek and kisses my lips before she spoke.

"Kash, I hope you know that I love you and I wish you would trust me. I understand how you feel about relationships—you don't need someone with all of the emotional baggage that I'm caring around. I just want to be here for you. I love you very much. Plus you and Michelle make a really cute couple," she ended it with a big smile.

"What are you smiling at Alexis? You know the life Michelle has led?"

"So what, that shit is the past. That girl loves you and only you. She ain't fucking with nobody down there. I know because I talk to her every day. Bet you didn't know that did you? Michelle loves you so much that she asked me to hold you down so you wouldn't be running around with these skank ass hoes. She said she'd rather it be me than them." Alexis was now up on her elbows.

"And what about her past life?" Alexis continued in

Michelle's defense. "Look at the life that I lead with other women, but that isn't stopping you from kissing me in the mouth." She was now waiting for a reply.

"I don't know what I will do with you women. Now shut up and let me taste my pussy on them sweet lips of yours." Alexis giggled and then gave me a long sensual kiss.

As we lay there together, we talked the night away. I shared with her the events of the day including the run in with Aunt Maggie and me feeling the presence of Grandma. Then to have all of that shatter by the run in with them boys.

"Kash you said you would set them boys up and killing them was the last resort. I listen to you—it sounds like your intentions are to kill them regardless."

She had me cold.

"It seems like this thing is more personal Kash. Whatever your reasons are, you know I'm with you. And this conversation is for our ears only."

"Now that's why I love you so much."

"Why?"

"Because you keep my secrets close to your heart."

TENDER RONI

CHAPTER 13.

"Maybe that isn't such a bad idea, Uncle Alejandro. The girls and I might take ourselves a well-deserved vacation."

"Yes, Yes, this is good. Then you can come to LA for a visit so I can meet this group of friends you trust so much. If they are friends of yours, they are friends of mine."

So I decided that the girls and I would take a vacation and go to Santa Monica for a week.

The following weekend, the girls and I, including my sister arrived in Los Angeles ready to party. We drove to Santa Monica then checked into the Wyndham Santa Monica. Standing out front of the hotel in our swimsuits unsure of where to go first. We walked towards the ocean to get a view. You would rarely catch me in such a way. But the body I was hiding under the sweats or jeans I stayed in was something out of a music video. Walking towards the water, heads were turning left and right.

"Kash you plan on catching you a man out here?" Kaylin said.

"I don't know—never had one before." I laughed out loud.

Yes, you heard right. I have never been with a man. Too busy about my bread to even think twice about a nigga. Alexis was standing there with her arms folded looking at me, but she wasn't smiling.

"What?" I threw my hands up.

"I will act as if I didn't hear that."

"Alexis, you know I'm not looking for no man like my horny sister over here."

"Hey, hey, I am not that horny. I just haven't had none in a while," Kaylin said with a shy smile.

"Too much information, Kaylin," I said

"Well it's true, I'm human," she defended. Hell, even Alexis be getting her some dick on the side."

"What? You know I like pussy Kaylin," Alexis screamed.

"Yeah, you sure do. I heard you two in the house a couple of weeks ago getting y'all swerve on," Kaylin burst out laughing.

Alexis blushed. She was embarrassed, thinking our little secret was safe. She looked over at Kaylin.

"Your nosy ass makes me so sick," stomping off.

Kaylin called to her, "Oh Alexis, it ain't' no secret." Alexis stopped dead in her tracks. She turned with her mouth wide open, looking at us in astonishment. All we could do was explode in laughter. This only made her more upset. Tia walked over. I was still laughing, and she was looking at me confused.

"What's all that about?"

"Nothing, Alexis found out that our little secret was out."

"I don't know what she's mad about. We all know you two were fooling around."

This made me laugh harder. Kaylin, Alexis, and Ashley walked off in the other direction. I told Tia to come on, I have a surprise for her. We walked back towards the hotel then down the sloped pavement leading to the lower level parking garage and hopped into the rental and rolled out. We drove down the strip, which was filled with people traveling up and down the sea wall. Women were in packs, dressed to impress, men oiled up in shorts with no shirts. All types of flavors. Never looked twice at a man before. Tia poked me.

"Girl put your tongue away. You ought to get you one. You missing out." I smiled as I continued driving. We pulled into another hotel on the strip, which was built in a fashion to where it extended out into the sea and pulled up on a line of Cadillac's that was out. Big grills, candy paint, plush leather insides, TV's belts on the rear with pop trunks, fifth wheels and all. I blew the horn and her cousin Jerf emerged from one car. Tia saw him and jumped out to greet him. It was all smiles and hugs. Jerf introduced us to the rest of his crew and then we all hit the beach.

***

The day went by smoothly. We were having fun, kicking it and doing our thing. Jerf and his boys had brought some jet skis to ride for the day. A few of them went back to their hotels to pick them up. We hooked back up with the other girls around the time the jet skis arrived, and everybody was getting a ride. Jerf and his boys were giving us girl's rides one after another.

Jerf called me over, "Say, Kash!"

"What's up Jerf?"

"Man I'm tired of all this chauffeuring shit."

"You know you like the fact that these ladies are all hugged up on you."

"You right," Jerf cheesed flashing his pearly whites. Won't you help a brother out and give these lovely young ladies a ride," he said pointing towards a couple of women, waiting for their turns.

I gave him a devilish grin, "I got you."

I made my way over to the jet ski and a dark skinned chick with a short haircut stepped over.

"Look," she said pointing. "My home girl wants to ride, but she scared because she doesn't know how to swim that well."

"Tell her I got her," I said. The chick walked over to her friend.

"Girl, come on here," the short hair girl said while pulling her friend from the crowd. And when she did, now being able to see her in full view. I thought I had laid eyes on a living angel. She was 5'6 with caramel brown skin, long black silky hair and a body so thick and beautiful that Halle Berry would be put to shame. She had a beautiful face with some rather large lips, but her lips made her even cuter. I guess me looking for a handsome chocolate man was going to get put on the back burner.

She walked over to me with her head down, all shy and timid. I stuck my hand out for her to shake it and she gently took it.

"Hello Miss, My name is Kash, and I will be your aquatic chauffeur for the day." That got a giggle and a smile out of her.

She looked up at me with the most beautiful brown eyes of hers and said, "Well, my name is Veronica and I pray that you keep me safe on this ride."

"Don't worry, Miss Veronica—I got you. All I ask is that you hold on very tight," I said with a sly smile.

"If you're my chauffer, how you going to flirt with me? Who said I was into women?"

"Perks of the job. I'm just trying to make you feel comfortable," I shot back. She laughed. "Now let's go."

Veronica and I rode for a while. Just feeling this soft woman touch around my waist and her soft full breast pressed against my back made me not ever want to return to shore. But I reluctantly headed back when I saw Jerf waving me in from the beach.

After we made it back in and I helped Veronica back onto the beach, I asked her, "So Veronica are you here with someone special? Male or female—or are you kicking it with your girls?"

"Oh, I'm just here with my girls. And you Kash," she asked giggling.

"I'm here with my sister and a few friends, and what so funny?"

"Kash, Is that the name your mother gave you?"

"No."

"Well, can I get your real name?"

"No one ever calls me by my real name, so it doesn't matter."

"Is that so?"

"Yes, it is."

"Well, I guess that means you won't be calling me because if I don't know your real name, I can't fuck with you. I like to know who I am socializing myself with."

"Well if that's the case, it's Keisha," I revealed with a smile.

"Keisha," she repeated. "I like it, see that wasn't too hard."

By now I was blushing and at a loss for words. When I finally got myself together, I asked, "So Veronica, when can I see you outside a group setting?"

"Well, I guess you can pick me up tonight since we're leaving tomorrow. I have to get back to work and to school."

"What school do you attend? The University of Minnesota, but I'm from Miami.

"Damn, what a coincidence, I'm from Minnesota"

"Well, this might turn out lovely after all."

"It just might Keisha. It just might," she said smiling.

After exchanging numbers, I headed back to the room to get a nap in before I was to meet up with Veronica later on that night.

***

While sleeping, the girls came in hitting me with pillows waking me up.

"Wake your ass up, little ole girl. It's time to go get our grub on." Kaylin screamed standing on the bed over me.

I rolled over, looked up at her and said, sorry sis. "I won't be joining tonight. I got plans."

"You mean you standing us up for some pussy?" Alexis angrily blurted out. .

"No Alexis, I'm not standing you all up for some pussy. I'm standing you all up for a very nice attractive woman," I answered with a smile.

"Yeah, she trying to get her fingers sticky," Tia snickered.

"Kash this is supposed to be a vacation for us!" Kaylin whined. "Not for you to be running around with hoes."

"If it was some dick would it be ok? I met somebody nice, and I want to kick it with her before she leaves tomorrow, that's all."

"I bet it's that little broad you had on the Jet Ski last," Kaylin shot back.

"So what if it is?"

"She looks sneaky ass fuck."

"Kaylin you tripping. How do you know how somebody is just by the way they look?"

"Women's intuition," she said flatly.

"You don't think I have that too?"

"You ain't no whole women," Kaylin said with attitude.

"Kaylin don't start this mother hen shit because I don't want to hear it," I told her as I got out of bed and headed to the bathroom to take a shower.

When I came out of the bathroom, they were gone. I called Veronica to see if she was ready. She told me to come through. She was staying in a hotel room about half a mile down the sea wall from the Wyndham were I was.

***

Veronica and I enjoyed our time together. We ate a light dinner while talking and getting to know one another. Being around her made me feel relaxed. She was the first women whose company I adored enough to let my guard down. Well, besides Michelle. I loved her company, but I had to be on my guard because of her background. We talked into the wee hours of the morning. We found ourselves on the beach, sitting in the sand, enjoying the breeze and listening to the sound of the waves. Then watched a beautiful sunrise, over the Pacific Ocean.

I walked her back to her room. When we made it there, I gave her a soft good night kiss on the cheek and told her that I would try to call her before she left. And if I didn't catch her I'll hit her up when I get back to Minnesota.

Once I made it back to my room, I found Alexis in my bed sleep. Not sure if it was for her benefit or Michelle's? I laughed to myself and sniggled up behind her with plans to sleep all morning long.

***

Once I woke up, I took a shower, then called Veronica to see if she had left yet. When I got a hold of her, she was crying and upset. Her home girls had voted to stay in Santa Monica a few more days. She needed to get back to her studies and her job. But didn't have a way to the airport. They had left her.

I told her I would take her. I called Tia and told her that I would be back later. I was taking Veronica to the airport. On the way to drop her off, we got a chance to talk more. She was surprised by my degree of intelligence. I was digging this girl. More than I had ever dug anybody in my life.

IN THE WORKS

CHAPTER 14.

I stayed in LA to meet up with Uncle Alejandro. I had a little time to kick it before Kaylin, and the crew drove back from Santa Monica. Uncle Alejandro and I discussed business, legal and illegal. Talked about how Kaylin was doing and how life was for me being back in Minnesota. I filled him in on what Kaylin and I were trying to do with Biotech and also the problem that I was having with the two crooked cops. He promised to lend whatever help was needed to remedy the situation.

Soon the ladies showed up, and after the initial introductions were out of the way, we had a good time. Uncle Alejandro fell in love with them all, especially Ashley. He later told me that she was an innocent in all of this and needed extra protection. I told him about her cousins, who practically ran her end of the business, and how Alexis kept them in line. We stayed with Uncle Alejandro in his mansion for two days, and then it was back to the hustle, back to Minnesota.

While we were out of town on our vacation having fun, little did we know Ashley and Alexis cousin Justin was getting busted by the cops. He had beaten his girlfriend Tameka down with a baseball bay. The idiot had dope on him when they pulled him over. They arrested Justin and took him down to the station where the case fell into the laps of them crooked ass cops, Jay-Jay and Winters.

His case fell into their category of cases—assaults, rapes, robberies, and murders outside of drug cases. They knew that Justin worked for Ashley and saw this as a prime opportunity to place a snitch on the inside of our crew.

Winters and Jay-Jay had it in their minds that they were going to take us down one way or another. Arresting my crew and I had become some kind of obsession for these two crooked cops. Justin gave them the perfect opportunity to infiltrate our organization and get the job done.

***

The next few months were uneventful as far as the streets went. We had established ourselves as the head bitches in the city and as hard as we worked. We played even harder. Being that Veronica was attending U of M, we went to all of their big games. We would meet up with Jerf and his crew, then shoot out to various events—boxing fights, the super bowl, All Star weekend and just about any event that caught our interest. You name it—we were there. I had never been the one to go off partying all the time, but something within me had changed. I had something worth living for now. I had Veronica in my life, and she made it that much more worth living.

Occasionally, I went to California to visit Michelle. How could I not, she was my bottom chic. Although she knew about my relationship with Veronica, it hurt her that it couldn't be her. But as long as I saved a piece of my heart for her she was cool.

Michelle loved me wholeheartedly, but she figured that she wasn't good enough for me because of her past. In many ways, I had felt she was right. What I didn't realize at the time was that Michelle was good enough for me and that I loved her. I recall one Friday afternoon when I received a call from her.

"Hello?"

"Hey, Kash."

"Hey boo, what's up with you? Calling to see if I'm still coming to your Graduation Party? Don't worry—I got you."

"Nah, that ain't what I called for Kash.

"Then what is it, Michelle?"

"Baby you know I love you, don't you?"

"Yes."

"Well your girl got a job offer in Atlanta, and I'm going to take it," she said wondering about what my reaction would be. "I know you wanted me to move to Minnesota when I got my Masters, but Kash I've got to do me. Plus I don't think I could live in the same town as you and not be able to have you as my world. You belong to someone else and to be seeing you living life with her. I couldn't take it, Kash. I just couldn't take it!" she said as her voice starting to crack.

"Why all of this now Michelle? I mean it's never been a problem for you in the past."

"Kash it has always been a problem for me! I just didn't want to lose what little part of you that I've been hanging on to!" Michelle said emotionally. "I'd rather have a piece of you than none of you! You're the only women that I have ever loved, and I die daily inside. Dealing with that love that I can never let fully grow!" Tears begin to fill the wells of her eyes.

She was crying by the time she got her heart felt feelings out, and I couldn't think of a thing to say.

I wanted to comfort Michelle. I wished I could reach through the phone lines, put my arms around her then let her know that everything would be okay. But I had no response to comfort this woman that I loved, yet fought not to reveal that love daily.

"Do what you got to do Michelle," was all I could manage to say, before hanging up the phone. I cursed myself for not being able to share my real feeling with her, and I knew I had hurt her by my actions. My pride wouldn't let me be the woman that she wanted and needed me to be.

Michelle graduated and moved on to Atlanta to start her new job. I provided for her whenever she needed me and still traveled there to see her and make love to her. We were dealing with our issues through our passion for each other. Unofficially Michelle was my girl too.

***

Meanwhile, back at home—I had moved Veronica into her apartment. She got a job working at Wells Fargo Bank. Veronica told me that she wanted to be able to pay her bills and not have to depend solely on me. I bought her a Volkswagen Bug to get around town and back and forth to school in. I had soon thrown myself into my relationship with her and my hustling.

My love had never been given away like this, and I was experiencing something entirely new. I gave my time and effort to our relationship. Maybe it was to cover up my secret longing for Michelle—I didn't know. In a lot of ways I was enjoying having Veronica in my life, but then there was Kaylin. She didn't care for Veronica one bit. Kaylin let her feelings be known directly to me and through her sarcasm towards Veronica. She would ask me all the time why my sister didn't like her.

"That's just how Kaylin is, towards mostly everybody." I would reply.

"Don't pay her any attention."

Life was good—I wasn't worry about the world. For the first time in a long time, I was happy and content. Until I got a phone call from Alexis to come over. As I approached her doorstep where her son was sitting, Da'Kwon jumped down from the top step and ran towards me.

"Aunt Keisha, Aunt Keisha!" he screamed.

I scooped Da'Kwon up and kissed him on the cheek.

"What's going on little man? You getting big on me, you taking care of your mama?"

He was nodding his head saying, "yeah, yeah."

"And how is your Grandma?" I asked him.

"She at work," he said. I turned my attention to Alexis.

"So Alexis, you in mommy mode, huh?"

"Yeah, you know I got to spend some time with my baby."

"Anyway, what the hell you call me for?"

"Oh yeah, Tracy didn't want to trick with the dude because he's a cop." Alexis whispered while leaning in close. I leaned in closer to her.

"What cop?" I asked.

"You'll never guess"

"Fuck, who Alexis?"

"Winters," she said then leaned back smiling.

I was shocked. My mouth was hanging wide open in astonishment.

"Close your mouth boo. You might catch a fly," she told me while stuffing one of my nuggets in her mouth.

I slapped her on her hand, "Hey big butt, get your own nuggets."

"Whatever. What you want to do Kash?"

"Shit, do you think Tracy down to put Winters on tape?"

"Hell yeah because I gave her ass a fifty for that info and told her that if she was willing to help out more on that tip, it was more money and dope to come her way."

"Aight Alexis this is what I want you to do. First, I want you to call that female you use to kick it with from Century Security and see if she can come up with some audio equipment." Alexis nodded listening carefully to what I was saying. "Then," I continued. "I want you to get Tracy ass and put her up in a room, somewhere in the burbs. Nothing fancy because I want this pig to come to her. Whatever Tracy wants, Tracy gets understood?

"Yeah, I got you."

"I'll call Ashley, Tia, and Kaylin to fill them in on what's about to go down."

"I got you. As soon as my mom's get home. I can drop Da'Kwon off." she assured me.

"Cool, call me when you get everything set up," I said walking to my truck.

"Bye, Bye Auntie Keisha," Da'Kwon screamed from behind the fence inside of the play area.

"Bye Da'Kwon." I hopped in my truck and sped out off. They say the devil works in mysterious was as God does. On this day, he was at work on me. Everything was going well for me, and then here comes revenge rearing its ugly ass. If only I had stopped and realized that at the time but I didn't. All other thoughts flew out of my mind. No thoughts of Biotech, none of Veronica, the hustle or nothing. Just revenge. I was about to be greeted by my guest for vengeance.

While I was planning my get back at crooked cops, they were gearing up to set us up with a plan of their own. By using Justin. The only problem with that was Justin couldn't get close to Tia or me, and Ashley was not enough. The evidence against her was minimal at best.

Justin provided a lot of information on our territories and us. He gave Winters and his partner a better insight as to some portions of how our operation worked. It was a foot race that neither side knew they were even running and all was getting ready to come head to head. My crew against them peoples.

NASTY BOY

CHAPTER 15.

Within a week we had everything set up and ready to go. We had Tracy and the equipment in a motel out in Lakeville. Tia knew the owner and slipped him a couple hundred to look the other way while we did our business.

We had everything all set up—Tracy was at the W posted at the bar where Winters stopped at on his way home. Tracy had explained that he always came through at the end of his shift on the weekends. He would have got dope from a young hustler or picked up what they had thrown down when they ran from them and used it to trick with Tracy. She said she was Winters favorite because she kept herself up, as opposed to the other girls who just let themselves go. Not only that but she already knew what he liked, and winters felt her head game was fantastic.

Tracy waited around for all of fifteen minutes then just like she had said Winters came through after his shift. He saw Tracy sitting at the bar. Walking over to her he sat on the stool next to her. He ordered a drink then turned to Tracy.

"Are we going to sit around here or can we take this meeting elsewhere?"

"We can head out daddy," Tracy said rubbing her hand up his leg then grabbing his dick. Tracy pulled out the cell phone we had given her and sent a text to Tia. Informing her, she was about to head out with Winters. "Daddy, you miss me," she purred.

"You know I did," he said smiling. They both got up and walked out of the doors. Walking to his car Winters ask, "Where the hell have you been Tracy?" Popping the automatic door locks then hurrying to get in the car. "I found me a rich trick I been working. He bought me these new clothes you see me in, and I got a room out in Lakeville. Now don't I look cute to you daddy?"

"Yeah you sure do," Winters said raping her with his eyes.

"Now let's stop by the store and get us some smokes and something to drink, then I'm gone show you how much I miss you. We going to the room, so I can fuck your brains out and suck that dick dry," She stated with a grin.

"You got it, mama," Winters pressed the accelerator and head for their destinations.

While Winter was in the store buying the items needed for their night of fun. Tracy placed another text to Tia and let her know they were almost to the room. Tia told her we were already there and waited for them to arrive.

The room was equipped with two microphones and two cameras. We had a room next to Tracy's set up with viewing monitors and sound recording.

"Okay, she down the street at the store. Everybody cut their phones off and don't leave the room."

Alexis, just make sure that cheap ass equipment your cousin picked up works. Tia said.

"Shut the fuck up. Alexis shot back.

I heard a car pulling up and cut their conversation short. "Both of you shut the fuck up—they're here.

"Alexis how are you looking?"

"Coming in clear as a bell boss," she whispered.

Tracy entered the room with her key and went to the bathroom to freshen up. We could see Winters fat ass taking his gun and jacket off. He then poured himself a drink.

"You want something to drink, Tracy baby?"

"Yeah daddy, you know I do."

"I got you," He said pouring their drinks. When Tracy left the bathroom, she entered the room dressed in cheap red lingerie she had purchased from Wal-Mart.

Winters eyes grew big, and his mouth flew wide open at the sight of Tracy. She was plump but not fat. She was a dark skinned woman with a cute enough face with large breast and ass. Tracy was one of those types of addicts that could smoke for years and lose no weight. She knew her role and knew how to have Winters eating out the palm of her hands.

"Take that dick out and let me see it, daddy," Tracy commanded.

Winters undressed and laid down on the bed so she could go to work on him. She went to the dresser, picked up her drink and swallowed it all in one gulp. Leaving nothing but a few ice cubes. Placing two cubes in her mouth, Tracy walked over to the bed and leaned over Winter.

She grabbed his small dick in her hand and blew her cool breath on the head of it, then opened her mouth and swallowed him whole. Tracy rotated the ice cubes around his dick with her tongue while lifting both of his legs into the air.

"Oh yes, Tracy! You know how I like it!" Winters screamed. "Give me what I want baby. Give it to me!" He begged.

Tracy stopped sucking and licked his dick up and down, continuing to push his legs into the air at the same time. She made her way down to his balls, letting her cold tongue slide down to his ass hole, where she blew her cool breath and stuck her tongue in it.

As Winter moaned, painted, and wailed like the bitch he was. Tracy reached for something on the nightstand. At first, we couldn't see what she had grabbed—then she moved it into view. It was a jar of Vaseline. She stuck her fingers into it, just as she moved back, placed his balls in her mouth and hummed.

"Oh yeah, Tracy! Give me what I want baby!" Winters yelled. He knew what time it was. She gave him what he's been pleading for. Tracy stuck her lubricated middle finger up his rectum and fingered fuck him in the ass. She rotated her finger in and out, watching as he went crazy, gyrating in sync with her rhythm.

In the next room, we all watched this disgusting freak session with shock and awe on our faces. The picture was coming in crisp and clear along with the sound and it was all being recorded. I was getting all I needed for my scheme to blackmail and destroy they ass. This was worth its weight in gold.

The sex session didn't last long. Tracy finger fucked and sucked him for a few more minutes, then straddled him and rode him for about two more minutes then he came and was ready to go. Winters got up and dressed.

Fully clothed, Winters pulled a small sack of dope from his pocket and threw it to Tracy.

"Don't smoke it all up, I don't know when the next time I might bust one of them little hoodlum bastards again."

Tracy removed a rock from the sack, put it on her straight shooter then lit it and took a deep hit. As the stench and smoke filled the room. She laid back on the bed and pleased herself with her fingers. Winters watched for a moment, and then gathered his stuff and left. Leaving Tracy there, masturbating to get her nut off as she did at the end of their dates.

As soon as he was out the door, Tracy jumped up and looked out of the window to make sure he was gone. Then she looked into the camera. "How did I do?" She asked with a devilish grin.

For her troubles, I paid Tracy three grand and set her up in California with an apartment and a job in one of Alejandro's restaurants. She turned out to be one of the best waitresses, slash prostitutes that Alejandro had ever had. His foreign customers loved this voluptuous black freak of a woman. I had to get Tracy out the way so that Winters wouldn't come back and retaliate against her for setting him up. I now had what I needed to turn these crooked ass cops world upside down. All I had to do was wait till the timing was right.

MOTIVATION

CHAPTER 16.

The grand opening for BT Drugs Inc. was scheduled for the next month. I wanted to at least get that out of the way before I implemented my plans against them crooked ass police. Kaylin was looking forward to the opening of BT Drugs Inc. with major excitement, and I was proud of the name. BT Drugs Inc. stood for Beatrice Taylor, our beloved grandmother. This legitimate business was dedicated to her. If only she was alive to see what her grandchildren accomplish. This would have been her dream come true.

Over the years, thoughts of my grandmother and the dreams that she wanted for her grandchildren had escaped my mind. But this day, I started to evaluate my options as far as what I was doing out here in these streets. Should I do what I truly knew what was right, give it all up and go straight? Hell, I could live comfortably off the profits from BT Drugs alone.

The day of the grand opening of BT Drugs in the media was out in full force along with all of the political bigwigs in

Minneapolis. You have the Mayor, City Council, business owners, the chief of police and state representative in attendance.

Kaylin was the center of all the attention. I stayed in the background and watched her proudly as she cut the ribbon on the front door of the new BT Drugs Inc. building.

"Welcome to a new day! A new beginning! To the new BT Drugs Inc. Of subsidiary of vital pro" Kaylin was saying as she delivered her speech to the cameras and on lookers in Attendance. As I listened on, I felt my cell phone vibrating in my pocket. I looked at the caller Id and saw that it was Ashley.

"What up, Baby Boo? Why aren't you here for the grand opening?"

"I was on my way until I got a call from my cousin Rondo and had to turn around to meet him. He mentioned he had something important to talk to me about," she said in a shaky voice. "Kash you need to meet me at your house right now! I had already called Tia and Alexis, and they're on their way," A frantic Ashley shouted.

"What is it, Ashley?"

"I can't talk about it on the phone, Sis. Please hurry. I'm scared and don't know what to do." She cried.

"Okay Ashley, I'm on my way," I assured her hanging up the phone. I was heading towards my brand new Range Rover when Veronica cut me off.

"Keisha, where do you think you are going?" She asked with a hand on her hip.

"Something came up Veronica—I got to go."

"What? Something more important than your sister's grand opening to y'all new company? And then you leaving me her with your sister and your bitch! Knowing that neither of them likes me."

Veronica was speaking of Michelle. She had come down at Kaylin's request to be a part of the grand opening. I didn't know that Veronica knew about the relationship with

Michelle. As I stood there glaring into Veronica's eyes, she must have read my mind.

"Yeah, your slick ass thought I didn't know?"

"Look, Veronica, I ain't got time for this right now. I got to go," I tried to walk around her, but she stepped in my way.

"Oh hell no, I'm supposed to be your girl and you just going to leave me here looking like a damn fool to go run the streets?"

I grabbed her by both shoulders and pulled her face close to mine. "Veronica, get the fuck out my way before you piss me off." I then pushed her to the side and went and got into my truck.

When I cranked it up, she went crazy, calling me everything but a child of God. A few people heard the commotion and turned to see what was going on. Michelle who was standing behind Kaylin gave her a nudge and nodded in the direction of my truck. Believe me when I say Veronica's actions didn't escape Kaylin's attention. I pulled off and left Veronica standing they're seething like an angry bear that had just lost its last meal before winter.

On my way to the house my cell phone rang. I saw from the caller id that it was Michelle. "What's up?"

"What's going on baby?"

"Nothing, I got something to check on."

"Must be real important for you to leave. I wasn't calling for myself. I was calling for your sister. She caught the little trade between you and your girl. She wanted to know why you were leaving.

You know she can't get away to talk right now. So she asked me to call," Michelle stated in clarification.

"Tell her something is up with Ashley, and I'll fill her in later. Tell her not to worry and to leave Veronica alone. I know she's probably going to check her the first chance she get."

"All right but you don't have to worry about your girl, I saw her standing down the street talking on her cell phone."

"Well, whatever she'll be all right call me before you leave okay?"

"Okay, bye boo."

I hung up, I was off to the house to meet the crew. When I got there, they were standing in the driveway trying to comfort Ashley. I jumped out and quickly walked up on them.

"Tia, what's wrong?"

"Let's go in the house, and I'll let Ashley explain it to you."

We went into the house and sat at the dining room table. All right Ashley. What has you all upset? I asked her.

"Kash I went to meet my cousin Rondo when he called me and said that he needed to holler at me immediately. He didn't want to talk on the phone. When I got there, he stated that they had heard from his dad that Jay-Jay and Winters we're building a case against us through me and one of my workers. He said that there's a snitch in my crew," Ashley screech and burst into tears again. I waited as Alexis comforted her and she quickly pulled herself back together.

"How reliable is this information?"

"If it came from Rondo and his dad, then it's one hundred percent reliable. Ashley interjected."

"But do we know who the snitch is?"

"No. But Rondo dad is Mr. Law & Order all the way. He said that cop's protects snitches even from the police.

"And from what Rondo was saying them cock suckers are going to make a move pretty soon," Alexis added. "We can't let Ashley go to jail."

"What am I going to do Kash?" Ashley begin crying again.

"You mean what are we going to do Ashley? I started pacing the floor, thanking for a minute. Ashley was crying while Tia was watching me.

I stop pacing. "It's that simple, we have to get them before they get us. We have to go ahead and use that tape that we got of Winters. I think that will be enough to back their asses up."

"Kash, I don't trust them bastards. They are two dirty motherfuckers. They found out you got something like that on them, they'll just try to kill your ass then to let you blackmail them," Alexis encountered.

"You let me worry about that my dear I got this."

"I hope you do Kash because I'm not built for prison."

That night I called everybody over to the house to discuss how it would go down. Tia, Ashley, Alexis, Kaylin and I were all having drinks trying to figure out exactly how we should proceed. I was deep in thought and had my cell phone off so that I wouldn't be disturbed.

"Now y'all, this has to go down in a public place, and I only want me and Tia to do the deal," I explain.

"Well, where the fuck we going to be at?" Alexis snapped.

"You know you're going to be in the shadows watching my back Alexis."

"And where am I going to be at sis?" Kaylin asked next. "I don't want you there! You got the company just opening and plus you're in the public eye now! I don't want to jeopardize you or the company."

"How are you going tell me some shit like that Kash? I'm going, and I don't care what you say," she shot back.

"No! And that's that!" I screamed. The entire room went silent. Kaylin frowned up and lean back hugging a pillow from the couch pouting.

"Now Kaylin and Ashley, y'all won't be there, and that's non-negotiable. Tia and I will do the deal, and then Alexis will watch our backs. Alexis, did you get a DVD copy of the tape?"

"Yeah, right here," she said pulling a cd jewel cover from her purse.

"Good, I want you to get that for me, so we can put it in an envelope along with the number of the throwaway cell phone that the bitch ass Winters is going to have to call. Get it to him tonight, so we can put it on the windshield of the car before the show starts." I initiated.

"I got you, boss," Alexis declared.

As I continue to go over the plans the house phone ring. Kaylin got up to answer it. Looking at the caller ID, she saw that it was Veronica. She responded to the phone with much attitude.

"Hello!"

"Um, excuse me Kaylin but is Keisha there? I've been calling her phone, but it goes straight to voicemail."

"Well, that ought to tell your ass something! Evidently, she doesn't want to talk to you!" Kaylin said with venom dripping from her voice and then continued. "And if you ever pull that emotional shit like you pulled earlier today at the grand opening. I'm a put my foot in your ass!" Kaylin screamed into the phone before slamming it down in Veronica's face, Kaylin was fuming.

I heard the whole thing. Kaylin angrily stomped back into the living room and plopped down onto the sofa. "Why did you do that Kaylin?"

"Fuck her Keisha, that bitch doesn't mean you no good know way," she spit out angrily.

I looked at Kaylin as if she was crazy, shook my head, and then continued with the conversation. I just figured that Kaylin was angry with me and taking it out on Veronica. I didn't have time to deal with that right now—I had bigger fish to fry.

TWO FOR ONE

CHAPTER 17

The video was delivered the next day as expected. I got a call from them peoples a couple of hours later.

"Hello," I answered.

"Who the fuck is this?" Winters spat into the phone.

"Think about it you dirty mother fucker. You know who the fuck this is."

"You little piece of shit!" He yelled. "I'm going to tear you a new ass hole when I find you!"

"You ain't going to do shit you fat piece of shit. Not unless you want a copy of that tape going to your boss, the newspapers, and the news stations. They would all love a story about a corrupt cop." I laughed into the phone.

"What the fuck do you want?"

"I want you to back off my crew. I want to know who your snitch is and I want all of the evidence you got against us."

I could hear him placing his hand over the receiver and muffled voices talking in the background.

"Look, I don't know if you're recording this conversation or not, so I won't say anymore over the phone. I'll give you a place and time to meet. Bring the originals and all copies. I'll have what you want," Winters stated.

"Do you think I trust your crooked ass? We meet where I say, and it's going to be somewhere very public."

"How do I know I can trust your sorry little ass?"

"You don't."

"When and where kid?"

"6 o'clock tomorrow night call me, and I'll tell you where."

"Just make sure you got what I ask for."

"Bye pig I said hanging up the phone."

"That little fucker got me by the balls. What are we going to do?" Winters ask Jay-Jay.

"It's time we will put our snitch to work and get us some insurance ourselves"

"What do you propose we do?"

Jay- Jay smiled a devilish smile and proceeded to explain to Winters what he had planned.

After ending my call with winter, I explain to the crew what was said and how we would proceed. Later that evening I took Michelle to the airport see her off.

"So it's back to Atlanta?"

"Yeah, baby," she said cupping my cheek in the palm of one of her hands. "And I didn't even get to spend any time with you."

"Yeah I know. I've got a lot going on right now say, and I don't want you getting involved in my mess."

"Baby, I'm still the same Michelle. I'm always here for you." She told me with love and concern in her lovely eyes.

"I'm happy to see that you are doing good for yourself. You always said that you were going to leave California and never look back. I'm proud of you boo. You've become a success."

"Thanks boo. But I don't look at my life as a success. Sure I clawed my way out of the hood. But a dream isn't any good if there is no one to share it with." She told me. Her voice was getting shaky.

"The things I did in my past..." she continued, "to get me where I am now has cost me an honest and pure relationship with the only women I've ever loved. She expressed as a single tear rolling down her cheek. I wiped it with my thumb then gently kissed her on the lips.

"Don't cry. You got me."

"Kash I have a piece of you. I have the scraps that Veronica throws away."

I put my index finger to her lips. "Come on." I took her by the hand and lead her towards the airport bathrooms. "Michelle, I can't get on the flight and make you a part of the mile high club, but I can come close."

"Kash, you're so bad," she said smiling. Letting me lead her into the restroom, which luckily was empty. We went to the last stall. I placed gentle kisses on her lips as I slid her skirt up to her waist. My phone kept ringing and ringing. Each time it would stop it started back up again. I pulled her panties aside and stuck my finger deep inside. Appeasing her sexually to avoid the subject of our love and relationship. She knew I loved her but fought that love daily.

We finished and headed back out. As we walked towards the security line, my phone rang again.

"Is that her calling Kash?"

I looked at her with resignation in my eyes, "Yeah."

Trying to be bold and firm, Michelle took a deep breath and then walked into the security line leaving me standing alone. As I walked away, I yelled, "Call me when you get there to let me know you made it safe."

She waved her hand. "Bye boo," I said walking out the automatic doors.

Before I could get to my car, something came over me— the thought that I might not see Michelle again. And if I didn't, I wanted her to know how I felt about her.

I ran back into the airport, but she was already through security and had gone to her boarding gate.

I called Veronica when I made it back to the car, and before I could get a word out, she started apologizing, asking me to forgive her. I told her that I'd pick her up from work and we can talk.

Making it to Veronica, we then headed to the hotel where the meet would be going down. This night with Veronica would be memorable to me for several reasons. The first being that it was our first time making love. The song "Feenin" by Jodeci was on repeat when Veronica entered the bedroom fresh out the shower wearing only a towel. I was naked myself, sitting on the edge of the bed. She approached me slowly, stood directly in front of me and pulled her towel loose. Letting it fall to the floor. I pulled her naked body to me and put her breast into my mouth. Sucking and licking like a newborn baby being fed for the first time.

Veronica gently pushed my shoulders with both hands, causing separation between us. Then slowly dropping to her knees, using the towel as a cushion. Looking up into my face, she started rubbing my breast gently, kissing softly down my stomach to between my legs. Using her arms to spread my legs, she placed her soft lips on my pussy—with her hot tongue, she twirled it in a slow circular motion. I couldn't help but moan from the pleasure. Ummm, Veronica baby, that feels so good. This went on for a few minutes until I felt myself about to cum.

"Oh shit, baby, I'm about to cum. I'm about to cum," I moaned unable to control myself any longer.

"No, not yet," she said abruptly stopping and raising to her feet. She pulled me up from the bed and laid down on her back. She spread her legs and drew her legs straight into the air, giving me a full view of her long and juicy flower.

"Keisha," she called to me.

"Yeah, babe?"

"Pull a chair to the end of the bed and have a seat," she panted out, rubbing her fingers in her moisture. "I want you to see this pussy that you love so much."

I did as I was told and pulled the chair directly in front of her at the end of the bed. Veronica started fingering herself with her middle finger, spreading her pussy lips so that she could plunge deep. I watched on wanting her more and more as I listened to the sounds of her wetness between her legs and moans from her mouth. Occasionally she would bring her finger up for air and start rubbing her pearl, rotating her hips, moaning louder and screaming out to me. "Yes, yes, Oh Keisha. I want you to eat this pussy.. After about 5 minutes of this, she came screaming, "I'm cumin Keisha, I'm cumming!"

As I was watching Veronica, I played with my pussy. She had gotten off and was still fingering her wet pussy with one hand and motioning for me to come to her with the other. She was now in full heat. I grabbed my double header. Veronica patted the bed instructing me to lay down beside her. I laid down next to her, and she guided my head to her breast. I placed my hand between her hot, wet thighs. I gently began stroking her. Pulling my fingers out of her, she then brought them to her mouth and started sucking them. I looked at her amazed at her freakiness. I'd never seen this side of her before. After putting her fingers back inside herself, she pulled them out and brought them to my mouth. I accepted them and savored the taste of her juices myself then placed a nipple in my mouth. Enjoying the sensation that I was giving her, I placed kisses down her stomach then making my way to her pussy, where I lost myself at the moment, plunging into e.

I licked, sucked, and lapped up all of her natural juices. She was moaning and squirming like a virgin having her pussy eaten for the first time. Gripping the back of my head her body shook as she screamed and panted her way into two orgasms back to back.

This was my first time performing oral sex, and I became lost in the new experience. Grabbing the double header, I slowly entered it inside her and then myself. With our legs intertwined, we slowly grind. Veronica then took my foot and started to lick my toes. We made love throughout the night. It was a passionate love making that I will never forget.

When I was asleep, my grandmother came to me in a dream. She was in the kitchen cooking something. I don't know what it was, but the aroma smelled just delicious. Seeing me standing in the doorway of the kitchen she waved me inside.

"Come on in babe."

"Grandma, is it you? Is this real or am I dreaming?"

"Yes it is me baby, and this is as real as you want it to be."

I went to grandma and wrapped my arms around her and buried my head into her chest. For the first time, I realized that I was a kid again. I hugged her hard and sucked in her familiar scent. "I've missed you so much. There has been a time I didn't know what to do and wanted to come to you for help like I used to do. But you weren't there. I couldn't talk to you, grandma."

"That's nonsense baby, I've always been there for you. And I stay talking to you. You just choose not to listen," Grandma stated.

"When Grandma? I never heard you."

"Yes, you did baby. You see Keisha—Grandma is always with you because you carry me in your heart. When you feel your heart tugging at you to do the right thing, that's me, baby. Now I don't have long so let me speak my peace. I love you, and you know the life lessons that I taught you. You got to take heed and be strong. But you got to realize that you can't control the whole world." Grandma explained.

"All you can do is make the best for you and look out for the rest if you can. You already know the answers to your questions before they are asked and you know what choice to make before it's even in front of you. Pray to God for the answers baby, and always remember what I told you—don't break my heart and cash is the root of all evil." She said as she floated away from my arms.

I desperately tried to hold on, but it was no use.

"Grandma wait!" I called to her. "Come back, grandma! Grandma! Grandma! Grandma! I was still screaming when I was awakened. I rose up, reaching for my grandmother screaming her name until Veronica brought me back to reality.

"Babe! Babe! Wake up!" she said grabbing me.

"Huh, huh."

"Babe, you woke up screaming for your Grandmother. Are you alright?"

"Yeah, I'm cool." Lay back down and get some sleep, I said calmly. My entire being was shook up. It was so real and strange. As I laid there awake in bed cuddled up to Veronica. I contemplated the dream that I just had. I observed life and the direction in which it was headed. Was the dream a sign for me to get out? Should I just walk away from all of this? Maybe I should but I can't. Not right now.

I had to save my crew and make them pay for the stress that they had caused my grandmother—which led up to her death. Maybe that was why she had come to me, to let me know that she's looking over me. Maybe I should pray to God for the answers. There's no way God would condone to what I'm about to do.

Lying in bed in a state of deep deliberation, I debated on these things within my mind until I finally drifted off to sleep again. This time I didn't dream. I only slept in deep fitful sleep that had me oblivious to all other existence. I was resting myself fully and comprehensively. A rest that I would need for the day that laid ahead of me.

WAR

CHAPTER 18.

The next day after Veronica had left, I called the crew to the hotel and went over the plan. Everything was set. We sent Ashley to her mother's, and Kaylin said that she would be at BJ Drugs. Around five- fifty pm, Winters was calling.

"What up fuck face?"

"When and where you little shit?"

"One hour, in the parking lot of Robbins Center on Broadway Avenue.

"If I ain't there in exactly one hour, wait. I'm still on the clock, and I have some business to tie up here."

"Don't try no slick shit cop, 'cause I'll send this shit straight to KMSP- Fox 9 and Kare 11 News on your ass."

"Cool your heels chick. I ain't gone' try nothing," Winters stated, a little too relaxed.

"Just hurry the fuck up!" I said hanging up the phone.

I turned to Tia and Alexis, "That cracker stalling', I don't trust his ass," I told them.

"I say we turn that shit into the news people anyway because whatever they got ain't gone' be worth a damn in court anyway," Tia reasoned.

"I feel you, but we got to see how much they got on us, so can't nobody else use it against us later. Plus, we need to know who this snitch is."

"You right. I'm just ready for this shit to go down."

"Me too," Alexis added.

"Check them burners and make sure the bullets are wiped clean, just in case something goes wrong," I said.

"We gotcha boss," Alexis stated, checking her AK with her extended clip.

As we prepare for the meet up, they were getting ready for us too. They had Justin with them and had him to call Ashley.

"Ashley, little cousin, where you at?" he asked.

"Look, I done ran my truck into this stop sign, on twenty-ninth and Sheridan Ave over North. I need somebody to come scoop me up before someone call the law. I have been drinking," Justin, stated feigning drunk.

"Boy your ass don't learn, do you? I'll be there in a minute."

"Hurry up, little cousin. I can't afford another DWI. I'm a walk to the Handy Stop"

"I'm on my way, shoot."

Jay-Jay grabbed the phone and turned it off. "You did good son, now run along."

"Y'all ain't gone' hurt her are y'all?"

"We the police stupid, we don't hurt people now get the fuck outta here."

It was a setup. Jay-Jay was waiting on Ashley at the Handy Stop gas station on the corner of Broadway Avenue north and Thomas Avenue north. There was so much drug activity that took place over there—it was the perfect place to pull Ashley over. He sat by and waited for her to show up.

Twenty minutes went by before Jay- Jay seen Ashley turn on Thomas avenue North. He pulled Ashley over and made her step out the car. He then proceeded to hand cuff her and put her in the back seat of his vehicle. After which, he called Winters and told him that he had the girl and was on his way. They weren't far from Robbins Center in Robbinsdale where Kash requested they meet.

Winters called me and told me that he was on his way. I told Alexis to get into her position, which was inside of a car that we had rented while Tia and I waited for Winters arrival. Little did I know at the time, Kaylin had plans of her own. She had rented herself a car, got a throw-away pistol, and was staking out the area. She refused to not be there for me. Kaylin figured that she had to look after me, even if I didn't want to be looked after.

All the pieces were in place. It was like high stakes game of chess. Everybody was thinking that they had the upper hand and getting ready to check their opponent, but the question was, who was going to be checkmated?

Winters pulled up about four parking spaces over from where Tia and I were standing.

"Showtime baby girl," Tia said to me, nodding towards Winters and touching her gun that was in the holster on the small of her back.

"Okay kid, let me see it," Winters demanded as he approached.

"Not so fast, where's the stuff you were supposed to bring?"

"What, you don't trust me?"

"Hell no, now stop playing games."

"I want to see it first. All of it."

I pulled a brown envelope out my back pocket. "Here you go." I said showing Winters.

"Is that all of it?" Winters questioned.

"Yup. We can exchange packages and go our separate ways. All these years that you been chasing my crew around ends. Right here, right now. Cool?"

"You got one thing, right kid. It ends right here, right now."

Tia and I looked at each other in confusion until we saw Jay-Jay pulled up next to Winters car. He got out and opened this back door. He then yanked Ashley out and brought her around to the car where Winters was standing. Jay-Jay had a gun pointed at Ashley side and was telling her to be quiet.

Ashley was crying but appeared to be unharmed. Tia went crazy when she saw Ashley.

"Let her go, man! Let her the fuck go!" Tia said as she whipped out her gun. This caused Winters to pull his—then I drew mine.

"Put that fucking gun down, Keisha Jefferson. I'll kill this bitch before your ass can blink," Winter spat pulling Ashley away from Jay-Jay.

"Let her go! Let her go! Tia screamed aiming at Winters' head.

This wasn't part of the deal Winters. What the fuck is you doing?" I said pointing my gun back and forth between Winters and Jay-Jay.

"No, you put your fucking gun down before I pop your punk ass," Jay-Jay said aiming towards us.

It was like a Mexican standoff. I was wondering where the hell Alexis was? Just as the thought crossed my mind, she appeared right on time. Alexis stepped up right behind Jay-Jay and Winters with her AK drawn ready to spray both of them.

"Let my sister go motherfucker before I ventilate you bitch asses."

Caught off guard, Winters spent around shoving Ashley towards Alexis and started firing. The first bullet hit Ashley in the upper back.

The force spent her around. The second bullet hit her in the chest, and she fell into Alexis arms.

"Nooooo!" Tia screamed. It was as if the entire scene was in slow motion. Tia fired at Winters hitting him in his right shoulder. He immediately duck behind his car and ran off towards the mall trying to dodge and escape the hail of gunfire.

Jay-Jay dove over Winters car trying to climb into his while firing at us. I was crouch down beside a car firing back at the same time trying to pull Tia down, but to no avail. She was shooting away like a mad woman at Jay-Jay and Winters. Winter took off running looking back at the spot where Alexis and Ashley were. Tia let out a scream and took off after Winters. Alexis was sitting on the ground with a bloody

Ashley in her arms rocking her back-and-forth. " it's going to be all right Ashley. I got you. I got you."

Out of nowhere Kaylin pulled up next to Ashley and I and jumped out frantically to check Ashley out. "Oh my god, oh my God." Kaylin pulling up and hopping out drew Jay-Jay attention long enough for me to get a shot off hitting him in his right arm. By then He'd gotten his car door opened and was retreating inside. Jay-Jay cranked up his engine and was pulling off as I unloaded my Glock 9mm trying to kill his ass. He sped away, swerving across the parking lot, car riddled with bullet holes and windows shot out.

I ran over to check on Ashley—Kaylin was giving her CPR as Alexis cried.

"Kaylin, is she alive?" I asked kneeling down beside her.

"Yes, but she's barely breathing. We got to get her to the hospital!"

"I got to go and help Tia—she went after Winters."

Hearing this brought Alexis out of her trance. "I got Tia, Kash. Just get my sister to the hospital, now go!" she said forcefully.

"I can't leave y'all!"

"Kash, take my car and go before everybody goes to jail," Kaylin screamed.

We could hear the sirens approaching in the background. I picked up Ashley's limp body and placed her in the back seat. Kaylin grabbed up my gun and ran to throw it away. "Go KASH! Go!" she screamed. "Get Ashley some help before she dies!"

Alexis had shot out behind Winters and Tia with murder on her mind and was approaching fast.

Winters had run through traffic across the street to the other shopping center with Tia on his heels. The whole while, they were exchanging shots. Near some restaurants, people were ducking and running for safety as shots echoed like cannons through the parking lot. A few of the stray bullets that Winters fired hit some innocent bystanders.

Running through the lot passing 41st Ave North, Alexis knew which way to go. The entire scene was chaotic. People were running in droves past her as She ran towards the screaming people running away from the gunfight. Winters fired a volley of shots at Tia, heading towards a residence area dashing between houses approaching an open park. Tia was surrounded.

"Drop your weapon! Drop your weapon, now!" Minneapolis Police officers yelled in unison.

Tia was in a zone. She heard the officer and saw their guns, but she wanted to make the man who'd gunned down Ashley pay. She charged toward Winters direction—they all opened fire on her, dropping her into a bloody heap. She was dead before she hit the ground.

Pausing at the sound of shots a block away, Alexis felt a tug at her heart. Then and there, she knew Tia was gone. She shook off the hurt and trudged on through yards leading to an apartment complex, a dead end where Winters had run into. He was kneeling on the ground behind a garbage bin in a panicky rush, struggling to put another clip into his gun. She crept around the bin and aimed as Winters got his clip in and swung his weapon towards her. He pulled his trigger before she could even react or get off a shot. Hearing the click, Alexis squeezed the trigger and fired off four shots. Two hit Winters in the chest, one in the injured shoulder from Tia, and the last bullet blew the top of his head off. Blood, brain, and skull fragments splattered all over the wooden fence. Winters 's body shook then went still.

Alexis stared at the dead officer's body. By the grace of God, she was still here. She looked down at Winters gun, it had jammed. Taking a deep breath, Alexis turned around just as some officers rushed passed the apartment complex with their guns drawn.

"Drop your weapon!" they yelled at her with their guns aimed.

Alexis was in a daze. She could see and hear the officers, but she didn't move. She stood there with her gun in hand, thinking about her sister and how she might be dead. She thought about how Tia was already dead and how her son would have to grow up without her.

"Drop the weapon, Miss! We won't repeat ourselves!" One cop ordered in the last effort to spare Alexis life.

Alexis dropped the gun and collapsed onto the ground crying. She was crying for Ashley. Crying for Tia, for her son Da'Kwon, and crying for herself. She knew this was the end of the road.

As Tia was killed and Alexis apprehended. I was driving like a madman, covered in blood, trying to get Ashley to North Memorial Hospital. Luckily it was down the street from where we were at off Broadway Avenue. As soon as I made it through the lights, the cops were on my ass. The sirens were on, but I couldn't slow down or pull over. That wasn't an option. I had to get Ashley to this hospital. She was unconscious, but I was still talking to her.

"Hold on Ashley, Hold on. We almost there. We gone get you some help and get you patched up," I was saying as I hit the corner turning onto Oakdale Avenue North. Police cars were behind me and now coming from nearly every direction. One tried to cut me off, I drove on the sidewalk to get to the emergency room doors and skidded to a stop. I quickly jumped out, opened the back door and pulled Ashley out. By this time the police were out of their vehicles with their guns drawn.

"Freeze! Freeze! Stop right there! Don't move!" they were telling me, but I kept moving, screaming for people to move out of my way until I made it into the Emergency room.

"I need a doctor!" I screamed. "I need a doctor! She's been shot. Somebody help me please!" I yelled in desperation. "Ashley, breathe babe! Don't you die on me! Breath!" By now the police were surrounding me with their guns still drawn, telling me to put the body down but I couldn't. All I could do was scream for help.

Finally, a doctor and some nurses arrived with a stretcher. "We got her, what happened?" The doctor asked me. "She's was shot—she needs help. She's barely breathing," I said. The doctor and the nurses took Ashley and rushed her away. The minute they did, the cops rushed me and brought me down to the floor hard and handcuffed me. Ignoring the fact that I was a woman. I was taken straight to Hennepin County. A quick search of the car, the throwaway pistol that Kaylin had was inside. She was in such a panicked and concerned about Ashley—she didn't even think to grab it when she left the car.

THE AFTERMATH

CHAPTER 19.

In the aftermath of what had taken place, Tia laid in the morgue dead from eleven bullet wounds. Alexis was arrested and charged with first-degree murder for killing a police officer. Ashley survived and was in the intensive care unit recovering from her gunshot wounds. Kaylin had gotten away from the scene with the gun that I had used to shoot Winters with and also the envelope containing the evidence that they had on Ashley—as well as the video of Winters and Tracy. Although we had made additional copies to be on the safe side and to use against them later.

Jay-Jay was being sought out for questions but was nowhere to be found. I guess the dirty dog had to go lick his wounds. As for me, I was being held without bond in the Hennepin county jail for Kaylin's gun and in connection with the shooting.

Ashley was released after two months in the hospital. She later confirmed with Kaylin what the envelope stated—Justin was the snitch. He helped set up the kidnapping with Jay-Jay. By this time Uncle Alejandro was calling Kaylin on the regular checking on the progress of our situations. When he got confirmation that it was Justin who had set Ashley up, he sent Juan down to personally find and kill him.

Justin went missing from his girlfriend Tameka's house one day. He was later found a week later floating in the Mississippi River with his throat slit and tongue missing. Tameka didn't grieve too much over the loss. She had never fully recovered or forgotten about the beating that she took from Justin with a baseball bat. Not only that, but Uncle Alejandro gave five thousand dollars to the person that gave him up. Tameka pocketed the money.

My gun charge was picked up by the feds and I wasn't charged for the shooting that took place in Robbinsdale. Which was only because the gun didn't match any of the ballistics from the slugs or the bullet casings found on the scene.

Kaylin had a copy of Winters video sent to the DA's office and to Alexi's lawyer trying to show that Winters was a dirty cop. But the crooked judge wouldn't allow it into evidence. Alexis was convicted of First Degree Murder of a Police Officer and was sentenced to life in prison. Even though the police obtained video surveillance footage from the hotel and the shooting at the Robins Center Parking lot. It was not use to help Alexis in her case, but used to charge Detective Jay-Jay with numerous felony charges, including Ashley's kidnapping. He was caught trying to give false statements to get out of the situation. But the cameras don't lie. Jay-Jay was sentenced to sixty-seven years and sent to the Federal Prison Camp Yankton. As for me, I was later sentenced to twenty-six months and sent to The Federal Correction Institute of Waseca.

***

Now that I've caught you up on my past let me update you on what's going on in my presence. I've been locked up for over a year and a half with less then a year to go. My time here is spent mostly exercising daily and keeping to myself. There are a few chicks here I know from the hood and a few that worked for me. Tia's Cousin Vanessa got here a few months ago and is serving a thirteen-month sentence for a credit card scam that she let some females get her caught up in. Vanessa is the only person that I kicked it with. We get together every day and walk the track. Even though it's painful, we talk about Tia and the times that we had together. Times I laid in my bunk nearly every night in disbelief thinking of Tia. It was all so surreal, like a dream or something. My homie, my friend, my sister was gone. I guess it felt that way because I wasn't there in the aftermath of it all. Instead, I was locked up in county fighting this charge.

Kaylin, Michelle, Jerf, and Vanessa were the only ones out of the crew to attend Tia's funeral. Uncle Alejandro also came down to pay his respects. Vanessa told me that it was one hell of a sendoff. He said it seems as if half the city was there. Of course, Ashley couldn't be there because she was in the hospital. I still talk to her almost daily. We console each other in our times of grief over losing our best friend. She also keeps me up to date on Alexis and what's going on with her case. Alexis writes me through Ashley who is also taking care of her son Da'Kwon.

Kaylin and I weren't seeing eye to eye on some things. She was letting my drug business go down into the gutter. She couldn't handle it all by herself. Tia was dead, Alexis and I were locked up, and Ashley was out of the game for good after what she went through. Kaylin could only trust and rely on a handful of people who were shaky at best. On top of that Kaylin was trying to get BT Drugs up off the ground, which was not working because she couldn't devote her entire time to the task. She had to split it up with the street business, my case, Alexis case and Ashley's recuperation. At first, the company didn't click because the new employees never worked together. The company had an extraordinary research team. But under the circumstances weren't producing as it should. This all led to no profit in the first year, and plenty of money being spent on keeping the business running and employees paid. It seem as if the dream of BT Drugs was slowly fading. The only extra expense that Kaylin paid out on was the purchase of the house we were staying in. She said that even if she lost it all, we would still have a decent roof over our heads.

Kaylin made the trip to see me nearly every visit except on days when I didn't want her and Veronica to clash, which wasn't too often because Veronica had graduated from the University of Minnesota and move to Atlanta to start her career. That was the excuse that I got most of the time for her lack of visit, then unanswered phone calls. Then there was Michelle who stayed true through and through. The only reason she didn't visit was to keep down the confusion between Veronica and me. In turn, she would just pop up on me once a month with Kaylin, and she would write consistently and send pictures.

While I was locked up, if you think that I had time to reflect on the things you're wrong the only thing on my mind was my cash. I had just started to build my empire, and it was crumbling already. From my legal ventures with BT Drugs to my illegal enterprises dealing with my drug empire. I had to get out and try to save at least one of them.

My time in federal custody was uneventful. I did my time and minded my own business. I formulated the plans that I could execute when I touch down in these streets and those plans had dramatically changed. Vanessa had gotten out and moved to Atlanta. That was all she had talked about when we were locked up together. "Atlanta girl. If you young and black it's the place to be." She said that everybody had relocated there and that it was going down real big. This played out right into my plans because I was hot as a fire cracker in Minnesota and couldn't go back and take reigns on the hustle tip. The other reason that I needed to go to Atlanta was to distance myself from BT Drugs and Kaylin. I had already partially smeared the well-known name when they linked me to the incident over in Robbinsdale.

The bullshit that went down was in the papers and on TV for months. Hell Vanessa told me that it made CNN. I needed BT Drugs to make it for Kaylin, myself and the memory of my grandmother. I didn't want to be selling drugs for the rest of my life. I wanted to go straight legal eventually. The other reason that I needed to go to Atlanta was that Michelle and Veronica. They both were there, and these were the women in my life who I trusted and love. They both already laid a solid and legal foundation for themselves or should I say for us, so I had no reason not to go. All I needed was to bring the heat. I have been keeping in contact with Vanessa the whole time after she had gotten out. Vanessa was her same old self. She had gotten with some of her Eastside homey's who had moved to Atlanta, and they just moved the party there. She sent me pictures and kept me up on the business side through Michelle. After I had informed Veronica of my plans to move to Atlanta, she was overjoyed but suspicious at the same time. Knowing Michelle lived out there also. Out of the hundreds of women Veronica knew that I could have, she feared Michelle the most. I guess she felt the connection between us. The argument ensued every other visit after I announced my plans to move to Atlanta.

"So are you coming to Atlanta to be with me or to be with your bitch?" Veronica asks during one of our visits.

"Look, Veronica, I ain't going to justify that question with an answer. You need to be answering me as to why you haven't been handling these visits. Plus your cell phone is always going to voicemail."

"I told your ass, I've been busy with his new job and I can't talk on the damn phone all the fucking time. As far as that other shit, you need to chill unless you want me to quit my job so you can take care of me full time."

"Damn Veronica with all the money that I'm kicking out to take care of you and your ass still not happy? Plus all that damn money you make on your new job as a photographer for a black magazine."

"Come on baby, cut me some slack," Veronica whined.

"Your ass can get some slack for right now, but when I come home, I don't want no shit out of you. You got that! You got that shit!"

HOME AGAIN

CHAPTER 20.

Before I knew it, it was the week before my release. I called home only to find out that Veronica had to be in Puerto Rico for a shoot. She didn't know that I was coming back and thought I was trying to get her to visit me and after the initial disappointment, I never let her know any different. I was released and greeted at the gates by Kaylin and Ashley. They smiled big and hugged me tightly before we walked towards a stretch limousine that was awaiting us.

"I love you, big sister. I'm happy that you're out and I'll see you later," Ashley said hugging me then walking off towards Kaylin's Range Rover.

"Where are you going, Ashley? Y'all not riding with me?" I asked.

"Naw Kash, we gone holler at you later little sis. We know this is your first night out and you need to get yourself together," Kaylin stated with a smile as she opened the back door of the limo for me. "Get in—somebody else is going to take a ride with you."

Before Kaylin could even finish her sentence, Michelle stepped out of the car dressed in a skin tight, white BEBE dress and some red bottoms. Her hair was styled in an elegant bob looking like a beautiful black goddess. I stood there with my mouth wide open amazed by her beauty. I have seen Michelle dressed up many times before, but never have I seen her look this beautiful. Michelle smiled, put her finger under my chin and pushed my mouth shut. "Close your mouth boo. Drooling is not one of your greater attributes."

"Come here, girl." I pulled her into my arms and planted a deep and passionate kiss on her lips.

"Well, I'll leave you two to it, and I'll holler at you in the morning Keisha. I love you, little sister," Kaylin said before retreating to her truck.

Michelle stood there in the door of the limo, looking like a box of chocolate with a ribbon wrapped around it. She extended her hand out to me, "Shall we?"

"Yes, my dear," I replied taking her hand and stepping into the limousine. She tapped the glass and directed the driver to move on. The drive was quiet at first. Then Michelle broke our silence by telling me that I had 72 hours to report to my federal parole officer in Atlanta and that I had a plane ticket waiting for me at the Minneapolis/Saint Paul International airport.

"That's cool babe, but where are we going right now."

"Don't worry boo. You know I got us a beautiful suite reserved at the Hilton Minneapolis St. Paul Airport. I am sure you want to change and get out of that prison gear. There are clothes in that bag," she directed my attention pointing at a black Louie Vuitton duffel bag on the floor. She licked her lips and watched as I reached into the bag and pulled out the clothes.

"Now let me help you get undressed," she said leaning towards me and starting to lift my shirt above my head. I obediently let her do so as we stared into each other's eyes.

The only time she took her eyes away from mine was to admire my thickness.

"Damn," she sighed running her hand across my hard abdomen. I had been gruesome with my workout routines while I was down and by her reaction, I got the desired results. Michelle continued to unbutton my pants, staring into my eyes the entire time. I let her slide my panties and pants off at the same time—I was instantly wet. She stared at me for a minute then haltingly decided to reach for my clothes. I grabbed her wrist and shook my head no. Pulling her into my Lap. I hugged her and kissed her while sliding my hands up her dress. She wasn't wearing any panties.

I laid Michelle down on the seat, still kissing her passionately. I raised her dress up around her hips as she speared her legs, eager for me to taste her honey. I stuck my head between her legs and began gently flicking my tongue across her wet pussy. She immediately grabbed my head, moaning and screaming in pure ecstasy. I tongued her sweet spot like a starved maniac.

Michelle bucked and rolled her hips uncontrollably rubbing her pussy against my face as if it was the greatest pleasure she had ever experienced. It felt so good to see her enthralled and into this. It turned me on to please her, I was lost in the moment. I licked and sucked on Michelle's pussy until her body started trembling uncontrollably I felt her muscles tightened up. She grabbed the back of my head and pulled it into her hard, screaming and moaning as her body shook in vibration. She came all over my face, exploding back to back. She then lowered her hips, and her body collapsed in the seat as she fought to catch her breath.

After regaining her composure, Michelle grabs the back of my head and kiss me deeply. After pulling away, out of breath. She guided me to a relaxing sitting position on the seat and kneeled down in front of me. I spreaders my legs, she stared into my eyes. She was the first women to give me head, the only women I have ever been with until Veronica. The women that turned me out. Until this day I have never been with a man. With one hand she used your thumb and finger to spread my pussy lips then began sucking me slowly, with her other hand she stuck her middle finger deep inside my walls. Flicking her tongue on my pearl, this was driving me crazy and exciting me at the same time. Within minutes I was about to explode. My body tensed up, and I grabbed her head. "Ah shit Michelle, I said about to cum. But she stopped instantly killing the sensation. Looking into my eyes, she pulled me to the edge of the seat, placing one leg on mine causing our pussies to touch and started to grind. Back in forth in circular motions. Between moans, she whispered

"Keisha I love you. I love you with my whole heart," she said.

"I know you do Michelle."

We moaned in satisfying pleasure after letting out a deep sigh, settling into a slow grind. Her warm moisture had taken me away. I closed my eyes inhaling deeply and lost myself in her scent. I actually loved this woman but would ever admit to it. Michelle meant more than I would ever say. She is where my heart truly belonged. But the roadblock in my mind about her past wouldn't let me give her my heart. Our souls were wrapped together as we moved our bodies in rhythm with one another. Oblivious to the rest of the world that was passing us by outside of the limousine windows. My body was at a loss as far as what to do. The feeling was almost too much for my mind to comprehend. Oh, how I missed the simple pleasures of having sex.

Every time I got ready to cum, Michelle would stop grinding. It was driving me crazy. This woman knew how to please, but she also knew how to tease. Fresh out of jail, I needed to let my juices flow freely.

"Michelle, please stop that, you're killing me. There's plenty more after the first one," I assured her as she picked up her rhythm.

Michelle kissed my inner thigh, then quickened her pace even faster. Rotating and grinding. All you could hear were our moans, animalistic pants, and original sounds of wet flesh.

"Oh shit, Kash! I'm cumming! I'm cumming!"

Michelle screamed out in a voice so musical to my ears that I couldn't contain my excitement. The feeling was so real and intense that it exhausted us both. We collapsed down across the seat, soaking wet with our juices and sweat in a tight embrace. Loving each other, this is where I belonged— this is where I wanted to be. Feeling, experiencing, loving and making love to Michelle.

Michelle and I had sex all the way to the hotel. It was a special night for the both of us. How special I didn't realize at the time.

***

Early the next morning I went to see Kaylin, Ashley, and Da'Kwon. After the social visit, Kaylin and I got down to business.

"So who do we have here on the roster to handle the work?" I asked.

"Nobody Kash," Kaylin said "I've been doing what I can do on my own when I have time. I got about six of the little homies from around the way that I'm fronting."

"That's it. Six dudes? You mean to tell me that these six guys are moving all this work?"

"All what work Kash? We done fell off big time. I told you I couldn't handle all this by myself and run BT Drugs, which is operating in the red right now. Plus I can't trust the little homies with no major weight. If I can't adequately supervise the business."

"Damn , how bad is it?"

"Bad Keisha, real bad."

"Well let me take a look at the books."

"I can let you look at the books for B.J. Drugs, but I stopped keeping anything written down about our illegal ventures when the feds started investigating us after you went to jail. They didn't find anything incriminating, and I wanted to keep it that way."

"Good move. Since that shit is so fucked up. I want to talk to you about my move. I already know that you don't want me to go to Atlanta to be with Veronica. But it is more to it than that. I've had Jerf down there checking on the business side, and I'm planning on setting up shop down there. You know I can't do shit here anymore. Plus I can get lost in a big city like the ATL. The fact that my criminal presence won't be anywhere near B.J. Drugs would be a good thing. You know I have Michelle down there to lean on if I need be."

"I know you can't stay here and hustle Keisha. But it might be time to throw in the towel and try this legit thing."

"What? Have you lost your fucking mind, Kaylin? Do you know what a mother fucker done lost? Shit, we got to get that back and then some. Fuck! BT Drugs is in the red. What are we going to do to get that out?"

"We can make it if we work harder."

"Listen to you Kaylin—you sound like one of them fucking squares. Is that what you're turning into on me, a fucking square? Is that what you want to be? A damn square? Your daddy was Kaymar mother fucking Jefferson, and your mom was the notorious Shanice Taylor. There isn't a mother fucking drop of square blood running through our veins." I spat with the spleen.

"I hear you, Keisha. But grandma was Ms. Beatrice Taylor, and she was a square. A God fearing, a loving square who taught us to love God first and ourselves. Not cash and power." Kaylin said on the verge of tears.

Her words got to me. But I maintain my composure. Deep down, I knew that Kaylin was right. That little old devil on my left shoulder wouldn't let me accept it. So with a deep breath and with resignation in my voice, I asked Kaylin. "Are you with me or not?"

Remembering what happened years earlier when she didn't ride with me and thought of the promises that she made to herself and my grandmother to always have my back.

Kaylin reluctantly agreed. "Yeah I got your back fool, but I wish you would think this thing over a little bit more."

"I already have Kaylin. I already have."

ATL BOUND

CHAPTER 21.

After getting things squared away with Kaylin, my next move of the day was to call Veronica.

"Hello," she said answering her cell phone.

"What up baby, where you at?"

"Keisha, is that you?"

"Who else?"

"Are you calling me on three-way or something?"

"No, I'm not calling you on three-way."

"Then how did you call? And from a Minnesota number."

"I'm at home Veronica."

"Quit lying."

"Girl, I'm not lying. I got home last night, and I'm about to hop on a flight to Atlanta."

"Oh, baby why didn't you let me know?"

"Because I didn't want you to mess up your trip to Puerto Rico. I understand how you love to travel and on top of that, the trip was free. So where you at, and most importantly, when are you getting back?"

"I should be back tomorrow night, and as of right now I'm in Miami because we had to move the last part of the shoot due to scheduling problems. I still don't know why you didn't let me know you were coming home. It's like you're trying to sneak and do something before you saw me," she said with a note of agitation and sarcasm in her voice.

"Veronica Brown, I ain't trying to go there with you so please, let's not."

"I'm just sayin'."

"You just saying what?" I asked angrily.

"Nothing Keisha," she said still clearly agitated. "Anyway, I'm going to call my brother Chaze and have him meet you at the airport and take you to our apartment. He has a key. So, when do you have to go see your probation officer?"

"I'll probably go today before you get back. Is my Jag at the apartment?"

"No, it's in storage. I'll have Chaze take you to get it—he won't mind."

"Are you sure?"

"Yes, I'm sure. Plus y'all got to get to know each other anyway."

"Well, alright then, I'll see you when you get back"

"Okay, love you boo, bye."

"Love you too. Bye," I said hanging up the phone with thoughts of Veronica's suspicious behavior in my mind. Man, I should have known that I would have my hands full with this woman.

I said my good byes to Kaylin and Ashley. I told Michelle that I thought it was best that we went back on separate flights, which she reluctantly agreed to. Then, I was off to my new life in Atlanta.

As soon as I got off the plane and stepped into the terminal, I placed a call to my boy Jerf.

"Hello, who dis?" Jerf answered.

"Your friendly neighborhood Spider-man nigga, what up?"

"What up, Kash Baby? You out in ATL already? I thought it was next week that you got out. Where are you at now?" He asked.

"I'm at the airport."

"I'm on my way to get you."

"I'm good, Veronica's brother is supposed to be picking me up, but if he doesn't show, I'll call you back and have you…" My words were cut off by a hand on my shoulder and a voice saying, "Ain't no need for all that there sister in law, the kid is here,"

Chaze said smiling with a mouth full of gold teeth.

"Oh, here he goes right here Jerf.

I'll talk to you later then," Jerf replied and hung up the phone.

Placing my phone in my back pocket, I turned to face Chaze with an extended hand to introduce myself, "What up Chaze, I'm Kash, but I guess you already know that."

"Yeah my sis got pictures of you all over the apartment," he said dapping me with one hand and holding his saggy jeans up with the other.

Now we sag in my town, but it's a slight sag just over the top off the butt. But the youngsters these days be sagging' hard, with the pants cuffed under their butts and all their boxers showing. I'll never understand it.

"But she doesn't call you Kash, she calls you Keisha," Chaze continued. "What's up with the name change?"

"Well, everybody else in the world calls me Kash, except for your sister. She chooses to use my government name. I guess she has to be different."

"Yeah, that's Veronica alright. Everybody around here calls me Stacks, but she the only fool that be calling me Chaze. That shit pisses me off sometimes."

"Yeah I know, but as you said, that's your sister."

"Yeah, that's her. Well anyway, is this all the luggage you got?"

"Naw I have a few bags checked in. I'll grab them, and we can dip. I know you probably got things you got to do."

"Yeah, I got a couple of things that need my attention, but we got time."

After I had grabbed my bags, we headed to Veronica's apartment. During the drive, Chaze and I talked and learned that he was an up and coming hustler who dealt in a little bit of everything. He loved and clung to his sister. He wanted us to be cool for that very reason. He told me that he knew that I was caked up, and said that he had my back if need be. I listened to him intently, offering the occasional reply so as not to be rude or have him think that I wasn't listening to him.

Chaze was young and had a lot of young boy ways. But he was a hustler and right about now I needed all the hustlers that I could get my hands on to push this work that I was planning on getting.

When Chaze dropped me off at the apartment and gave me a key, I told him that I would be calling him later to take me to the storage to pick up my Jag.

The rest of my day was uneventful. I went and got my car, then got Chaze to drive me to see my parole officer who was too busy and overworked even to remember me or notice me. That was right up my alley.

After Chaze dropped me back off at the apartment, I met up with Jerf. He came to swooped me up and showed me the layout of the city and his new trap spots he had set up. He had a few places, but nothing major. Jerf hustle was getting work from his boys at Cali prices and reselling it to the locals at a higher rate. He knew that whatever I would be fronting him would be unlimited. Knowing that Kaylin and I had money and that Uncle Alejandro was my connection.

Finally relaxing since I landed in Atlanta, my thought was interrupted by the sound of keys and the front door opening. "Keisha!" Veronica called out excitingly as she entered the apartment.

"I'm in here baby," I responded from the living room.

I stood to meet the eyes of the women whom I had lusted over for almost two years. Veronica smiled a big smile when she saw me, and I opened my arms to greet her. She ran towards me, and as I smiled and braced myself for a hug, she greeted me with a hard slap across my face.

I stood there—astonished at what Veronica had just done.

"Girl your ass got out of jail the other night, but you didn't bother to call me then!"

"What the fuck you talking about?"

"Yeah, mother fucker, I called the prison and found out when your sneaky ass got out. Then I spoke to your parole officer—you didn't get out last night. You been out a whole 48 hours. So where the fuck you been? Naw, what the fuck you were doing the night you got out of jail that you couldn't call me? The woman you suppose to love!"

"You tripping."

"Naw motherfucker, you tripping for thinking I'm stupid. Now tell me, what bitch got some coming home sex? Tell me!" she screamed.

The anger and frustration with this women had built up and came to a head so quickly that I lost it for a second. Before I knew it, I had slapped Veronica with the quickness of a cheetah, grabbed a fist full of hair and yanked her head back.

"Look bitch," I whispered with anger. "I didn't come home to have you snapping on me when you are feeling insecure and fucked up. Now get your motherfucker mind right before I get it right for you," I growled forcefully pushing her away from me.

She stumbled barely catching her balance, then stood there shaking and crying. "Bitch don't nobody put their hands on Veronica Brown and not live to regret it.?" She yelled with as much menace and venom as I had ever heard come from a woman's voice. She wiped the tears from her face and stomped upstairs, slamming the bedroom door. At that moment I knew that if I didn't reign her in, she was going to be a major problem.

TROUBLE WATERS

CHAPTER 22.

Veronica and I rarely saw each other after our little fight. Either she was working, or I was out with Chaze or Jerf checking out the drug scene. If not there, I was at the rental car company that I had set up for myself as a legitimate front. My parole officer would call or drop by while I was busy with work. This cast out all suspicion from me when it came to my illegal activities. I would also sneak off to see Michelle every now and then. We would hook up at her place or at the Marriott near the car rental company. One day Chaze pulled up to my car rental company as Michelle and I were leaving. Not knowing that this was my other woman, he followed us to the hotel just a couple blocks away. While I paid for the room, Michelle stood behind me. Chaze must had been standing right outside the lobby doors watching and waiting out of sight.

Once I got the key, I signaled for Michelle to come on. Walking down the hall to the room, which was on the first floor. We entered room 112. Just before the door closed, Chaze stepped in.

"So what do we have here Kash? You creeping on my sister?"

I noticed how Chaze was always checking me out from the corner of his eye around the house. But knowing I was sleeping with his sister, he stayed away.

"Come on in Chaze." As Michelle slowly undressed, Chaze watched.

"I know you been looking at me Chaze—I know you want to see what has Veronica all in her feelings. Have I ever mentioned that I never been with a man before?" Chaze eyes amplified, it was all registering in his head that a man has never penetrated me. I begin to undressed then laid on the bed. I placed one leg over my head. Before we knew it, Chaze was undressed with his dick in his hand stroking it. To my surprise, it was a nice size being the first one I ever seen. He watched for a moment—his eyes stayed on mine. As Michelle licked and slurped on my pussy—with every moan, Chaze walked closer keeping a steady stroke until he was at the edge of the bed. He tapped Michelle on the ass signally her to move over, Chaze crawled on the bed and took Michelle spot. Chaze begins slowly placing soft kisses on my pussy admiring it. Then he begins to trace it with his tongue. He wasn't use to seeing a nicely waxed pussy. Michelle leaned over him and started sucking his dick. This went on for a few more minutes until he felt his knees weakening. He was amazed by Michelle dick sucking skills for a woman that was never seen with a man. Pulling from her mouth, he leaned up to enter inside me. I was nervous for a min, but it was no turning back, his head broke my barrier, and he slowly slid inside. I took deep breaths as he began to stroke me. All this time I been missing out on another amazing feeling. We went at it for what seemed like hours. Taking turns between Michelle and me, we all fell out in the bed with no energy and out of breath. So much was going through my mind. I didn't feel one ounce of guilt after Veronica brother broke me in. We all got up and took turns showering then we all left and went our separate ways.

Chaze barely came around the house after that day. Veronica and I relationship were becoming more strained. We hardly went out together or even talked to each other for that matter. We made love when either of us was in the mood, but it seemed more like a duty to be performed for the other. Then "I love you" were dry and devoid of emotion. Hell, the relationship itself was devoid of emotion except when she couldn't contact me immediately and suspected something. That's when the jealousy and the rage would rear its ugly face. But it never got to a physical state. Most of the time she would question me then offer a snide remark or comment towards the nature of my infidelity. I would tell her to stop tripping and let her know that I didn't want to hear it. Her reply in return would always be something smart.

I didn't have time for Veronica with her ranting and raving. My mind was on my money, and my new come up. But little did I know to keep my life drama free would be to no avail. The drama would always come in one form or another.

Over the next few months, I begin to get thicker, my skin was glowing, and I was emotional all of a sudden. I was not my usual self. I was at Michelle's house talking on the phone with Alexis who had called from prison when more drama started.

"Yeah, I got the money you sent," Alexis said.

"Good. Ashley told me that the lawyers seem like they are dragging their feet so what do you want me to do about that?

You know I'll fire their ass in a minute and go with somebody else."

"Keisha, don't do that. The lawyers are doing their jobs. It's just the legal process, and you know how that shit is. Especially with suspected cop-killers."

"I feel you, but I'm not trying to see them crackers fry you like a piece of the kernels secret recipe either."

"Keisha I don't want to talk about that. Let's talk about you and what's going on in your life. I hear all this lawyer talk all day long in here. I want to call home and hear something positive and uplifting for a change. What's this I hear you putting on weight? You letting that sexy get away from you down there?

"Yea, I picked up a few pounds but nothing to the extreme. Just need to lay off the biscuits." The thought of biscuits made my stomach twist and before I knew it, what I ate earlier was on the floor. Michelle was coming out the room.

"Kash that's the third time today you lost your stomach on my floor," Michelle screamed in disgust.

Alexis on the phone started to "oooh." "Kash," Alexis said with curiosity. "The weight gained, the throwing up. Let me find out you finally got some sausage inside you?"

Then it dawned on me. I haven't had my cycle since I slept with Chaze. All the signs were there, the growing appetite, weight gain, and the mood swings.

Michelle looked at me with the question Alexis was thinking but didn't directly asked. After she had cleaned up my mess, she walked out the door giving me a stink face.

Alexis and I spoke a little while longer before I said good bye and ended our call. I sat there staring off into space. Could I be pregnant with my first child? If so this was going to change my life dramatically. I started contemplating on the signs that I have been having. Soon my thoughts drifted to fantasies of my future child and doing things together with him or her. Then the thought of my grandmother. She would not be here to see her first great grandchild being born. Then my thought drifted back to reality. To Veronica and what her reaction to all this would be. That situation would not be a pretty one. Then breaking the news to Chaze. Of all people I would be the one to get knocked up. I laid back on the couch thinking about everything and fell asleep. Hours later, I was awakened by a gentle kiss on my lips. I smiled at Michelle, she handed me a bag and told me I needed to take this test.

"It's no secret, we both know your pregnant."

I got up and went into the bathroom to pee on the stick. I placed it on the counter then walked out. "Five minutes right?" I looked at Michelle with confusion on my face. Michelle smiled with a panicked expression. We waited patiently for the time to be up. Then Michelle went into the bathroom and came out fear written all over her. Then asked me what was I going to do?

"I don't know. With all that's going on right now, I don't know."

"Are we going to have this baby?" Michelle stated with discourage written all over her face. Then she hung her head down.

"Michelle I…"

"Wait," She interrupted me before I could get a word out.

"This is your decision being made here. And I know your girl, she would never accept this child."

I sat there staring into her teary filled eyes. She was more hurt and disappointed than I was. I hugged her tightly. Right then and there in the back of my mind. I came to the realizations that the relationship between Veronica and I was coming to an end. I knew what I had to do, just wasn't sure if that was what I wanted to do. I had to talk to Veronica. I had to be honest with her and lay all my cards out on the table. I felt that I at least owed her that much. Then I needed to tell Chaze. And depending on his reaction, I would proceed from there.

As I was going over the conversation in my mind as to what I was going to say to Veronica, my cell phone rang.

Getting up from my lap, Michelle said, "I'm going to get in the shower, will you be here when I get out?"

"Yes, I'll be here," I said as I looked at my caller ID, then answered the phone.

"Hello?"

"Hello to you my friend, Keisha," Uncle Alejandro said with humor in his voice.

"What's up, Unc?"

"Well my friend, what is up is you."

"Oh yeah? I'm listening."

"You know, no phone conversations. A representative of mine is in your town. He will meet you at your apartment at 9 pm sharp. He'll have the message for you, and you deliver your terms back to me through him. Agreed?"

"Alright Unc, I'll holla at you later."

"Yes, talk to you later."

Getting off the phone, Michelle walked into the room in a robe. We talked for a while longer, I got up and headed back to the apartment to meet Uncle Alejandro's messenger. I was running kind of late, so I called Veronica from my cell phone and told her that I was expecting company. I told her to make him as comfortable as possible until I got there. But the drama queen just had to make a fuss about it.

"Who you got coming over to my house?" She asked annoyingly.

"First off, it isn't your fucking house and second I can invite whomever I damn well please over there. You just do what the fuck I asked you to do before I come there and show your ungrateful ass whose house it is!"

"Is that a threat Keisha?"

"Veronica please stop playing with me.

"You just keep your little drug business out in the streets."

"Just do what I asked you to do and don't leave because after my peoples bounce, I got something I need to talk to you about."

"Whatever Keisha," she snapped. Hanging up the phone before I had a chance to respond. This woman knew how to get under my skin. This gave me the nerve to tell her that I was pregnant.

THE COME BACK

CHAPTER 23.

When I arrived at the apartment, there was a rental car in my space. I assumed it was Uncle Alejandro's messenger. When I entered the apartment, I was surprised to see Juan himself sitting there. He stood when I came in, and we cordially shook hands and greeted one another.

"Hello, my friend Keisha."

"What's up, Juan. I'm surprised to see you here."

"Yes, yes. I was down this way taking care of something else for my father with my cousins.

"Umm excuse me," Veronica said sassily, rising from a side chair. I hadn't even noticed her sitting there when I came in—probably because miss loud mouth was so quiet.

"Oh sorry, Juan. This is my girl Veronica. Veronica this is my friend Juan." I introduced them.

"Yes Kash, We already met," Juan said with displeasure in his voice.

"Yeah, we sure did. Now if you don't need me to play little miss hostess no more. I'm going up stairs." She said stomping off. Before she left the room, neither one of us noticed that she pressed the talk button on the intercom system. A box was located on the wall in nearly every room in the apartment.

I looked at Juan with an exasperated look after Veronica was gone and then shrugged my shoulders.

"No, Kash, that is not your average women. She is a viper! A Snake! And I don't trust her." He admitted.

"Come on Juan, I know you and I haven't gotten along in the past. But dude that's no reason to insult my girl."

"No Kash, I don't say these things to offend you. What differences we had in the past are just that, in the past. My father trusts you like he did Rico. So I trust you also. You have proven yourself to be trustworthy, but I tell you these things for your own best interest. And for the benefit of my father and me. Because if anything were to happen to you, we lose money also. Not just that but I care about you my friend, and it would break my father's heart if he were to lose such a close friend.

"Well thank you for your concern, Juan. But I got Veronica. Hell, she might be a distant memory after tonight."

"How is this, my friend? Do you plan to put in some wet work on your woman?" He asked.

"Naw man you tripping. Forget about that. Let's get down to business before she walks in and hears your loco ass talking about some wet work." I said humorously.

"Yes, let's get to it. We have a package arriving

tomorrow. It will be three hundred kilos of some of the purest cocaine this town has ever seen. And with your sister's help, that can easily be turned into four hundred kilos. You will own this fucking city. You see we have not expanded our business to Atlanta because we had no true representative that we could trust."

"So that's where I come in," I interjected.

"Yes, Kash. That's where you come in. Atlanta is a major city that is doing a lot of dope business now. This is a place where all the major movie stars and rap stars come to live. Where they come to play and where they go, everyone follows. The models, the wannabes and the dope boys that want the same status and fame of the movie, rap, and sports stars have. They don't want it later and through hard work. They want it now and fast. Do you see what I'm saying, Kash?"

"I got it baby boy. It's a marketing strategy. You give these dudes a chance to ball like the stars and with the stars. As you know, everybody wants to be somebody."

"Yes, this is true. Everyone wants to be rich, and we supply the people the means to become so."

"I see what you're saying. So when and where will this life altering shit be taking place?"

"You have a separate garage and storage warehouse across town that you use for your rental company. That'll be as good a place as any. They will arrive at midnight. I'm assuming you will handle the stash houses or should I have a couple of our people come in for the job?"

"I can handle that. I got my boy Jerf down from Cali."

"Okay. But listen to me, Kash. I remember Jerf, the party boy. This is no joke. No time for fun and games. For what is coming in, people would kill their own mother. So you have to be very careful. Plus I've also checked into your new crew."

"What new crew?" And how do you know who I hang with?"

"It's mainly Jerf and this new kid Stacks. The snake woman's brother. He has a reputation for being a stick-up boy and something of a hot head. I don't have a problem with Jerf. Just keep his flamboyant habits in check. Now this Stacks dude. He worries me."

"I got Stacks, Juan. When this kid and his crew start making this big money, all that small time shit is gone fly straight out the window,"

"Ha! They have their hands in big money as you say. Did you know the little bastard had his hands in a couple of bank robberies?"

"Naw, I didn't know that. But so what, as long as Stacks and his crew can handle the weight I'm about to lay on them. Fuck the rest."

"I hope you are right my friends. I hope you are right."

During the time of Juan and I meeting, what I didn't know was that Veronica was upstairs in the bedroom listening to everything that we discussed. I saw Juan out to his car. I came back inside to find Veronica in the room just hanging up the phone.

"What's up shorty?" I asked playfully.

"Nothing just got off the phone with Chaze."

"Oh, yeah? What he talking about?"

"Nothing. He asked what you were up to and wanted to come over. I told him now was not the right time, that we needed some us time. So what was it that you wanted to talk to me about boo?"

I walked over to the bed where she sat, grabbed her hands and look into her eyes. "Veronica, you know I love you, don't you?"

"Yes Keisha, I know you love me—even though things haven't been the best lately."

"Yeah, but things don't look like they're going to get any better anytime soon."

"Why would you say that Keisha? What's wrong?" she asked with a frightened look on her face.

"Well, it depends on how you look at it. But I need to know something first."

"What?"

"Could your love for me overcome any obstacle that came our way?"

"Yes Keisha, you know I love you," she released my hands and hugged me tightly. I could feel her heart pounding.

As she laid her head on my shoulder, embracing me. "I hope so Veronica because only our love can get us through this."

"Get us through what boo?"

I took a deep breath. Veronica, I'm pregnant by Chaze. I could feel her body stiffen and grow motionless. For a second I wondered if she was still breathing. Veronica gently pulled away from me. She looked at me with tears welling up in her eyes and slapped me as hard as she could. I couldn't do anything but take it. I did her wrong and hurt her badly. After staring at me silently for a few moments, she finally asked me. How? When?

"About two months ago. He followed me creeping to get a room with Michelle."

"I knew it. You cheating as bitch. I knew you were still fucking that bitch."

"Roni babe." I started before I was cut off.

"Don't Roni babe me mother fucker," she said. I knew his trifling ass was going to try it. Always wanting to hang around since you got here.

"Veronica calm down and take it easy."

"Take it easy?" she said exaggerated with her finger in my face. "Take it easy? Keisha, you come up in here telling me you got pregnant by my brother and you expect me to calm down. Bitch, please."

"You see this is the type of shit that I was talking about."

"Talking about what and to who?"

"Nobody, I'm just saying."

"What?"

"Nothing Veronica." In a calm, soft voice I asked with authority. "What you gone do?"

"What do you mean? What am I going to do?" She asked in a low whisper—her eyes filled with tears.

"I mean what are you going to do about us and this situation that has come up?"

Looking up at me, tears started to stream down her cheeks, she let out a big sigh. "I'm not going anywhere Keisha. I love you too much to let something like this take you away from me and cause a raft between my brother and I. I don't want to lose what we have," she whisper.

"Are you willing to accept my infidelity and swallow your pride so that we can make it through this?"

Sniffling, Veronica wiped the tears from her eyes and nodded "yes."

She jumped up and hugged me tightly. "I love you Keisha, you're my soul mate, and I am willing to do what I got to do for you boo."

I hugged and embraced her back. Wanting to believe her. I yearned to believe her, but for some reason, something in the back of my mind was warning me not to accept her words wholeheartedly. I took it at face value, ignored my intuition and went against my better judgment. I made myself take her words.

"I love you, Keisha," she cried on my shoulder.

"I love you too," hugging her tighter.

Little did I know then that Veronica was not going to let this act of betrayal go unpunished. She was an excellent actress and has done her job well. As far as convincing me of her false sincerity.

They say, "Hell has no fury as a woman scorned." And I was soon about to find out just how much fury a scorned woman could unleash.

VIBES

CHAPTER 24.

The next morning I called Kaylin to see how things were going with B.J. Drugs. She answered the phone and I immediately felt her low energy.

"What's up sis?"

"Hey, I was wondering when you were going to call."

"I know you've been busy so I didn't want to disturb you. So tell me how are things progressing on the home front?"

"I don't know if I would use the word "progressing." Regressing would be more like it."

"What's wrong Kaylin?"

"It's nothing really—it'll work itself out."

"What?"

"Keisha, I don't want to worry you with any of this, especially with all that you have going on now."

"What do I have going on that is so important that I can't lend a hand or ear to my big sister?"

"My new niece or nephew is very important, Keisha."

"Oh, so you know about this too."

"Well, Michelle told me about it last night after she had you take a test. The first time you get some dick, and you get pregnant. Wow."

"I can't wait to talk to her big mouth ass.

"Oh, did you know that Alexis lawyer said that she has a real good shot on her appeal?" Kaylin asks excitedly.

"Naw, she ain't mention shit to me about it."

"I think she probably wanted to wait until she had some concrete news before she told you. You know that girl loves you to death."

"Yeah, I know. "

"And you know that we've been talking and we think that you should come back to Minnesota to raise the baby. That way you would have some help."

"Don't start this with me. What about Veronica? Where does she stand in all of this? Or have you forgotten about her?"

"Look Keisha—I'm just saying."

"Saying what?"

"Nothing, I'm just gone pray about the situation."

"Anyway, what's going on with you?"

"Nothing, just doing my church thing. That's where I'm at most of the time."

"So you done started back going to church. Which church are you attending?"

"Grandma church."

"Oh yeah, that's good. Say a prayer for me but that isn't what I was talking about when I asked what's going on with you. I want to know what the problem is that you said would work itself out. And personally. I haven't ran into too many problems that just work themselves out."

"It ain't nothing," she claimed obviously hiding something.

"Tell me, Kaylin. I ain't got time to play theses fucking games with you. I got too much on my damn plate, and you're frustrating the situation more."

"Okay, okay, stop tripping. Biotech and the bank are putting pressure on me to catch up on my loan payments. Biotech is now trying to make a move to buy my debt from the bank. Then they could put a lien on BT Drugs to gain interest in the company. Something they wanted from the very beginning."

"So what are you saying? That we're about to lose BT Drugs?"

"Hell no that shit ain't happening. All the more reason for me to do what I got to do on my end."

"But Keisha, I don't feel right about you being down there. I feel that the devils in the mist down there with you. I feel it in my spirit."

"Aw shit. Here you go getting all holy on me. If the devil is in the mist, he better back the fuck up."

"Please Keisha, let me call Mr. Clark to see if there is something he can do to help us out?" She pleaded with reason.

"Kaylin, are you crazy? Clark works for the bank that is trying to fuck you. Hell, he has an investment in all of this. Don't you think he knows what's going on with his investment?"

"But Keisha," she uttered in near tears.

"But Keisha my ass! I don't want to hear shit else about it. Just do what you do and get ready to send me a mixture of yeast to make this bread rise. I got this. We ain't about to lose BT Drugs."

"Aight Keisha," she replied with resignation.

"I got this, Kaylin. Smile, we about to be on top of the world."

"I love you Keisha."

"I love you too sis," I replied before hanging up the phone. I took a deep breath and then punched in another number.

"What's up?" a male voice answered.

"What's going on with you," I asked.

"Shit just got in the house from being in these streets. But what's up? You calling for round two?"

I ignored his goofy ass question. "Have you spoken to your sister?"

"Yeah, earlier."

"So then you know what this call is about?"

"Kash, what's up? Did you tell her about our encounter or something?"

"Chaze she knows, and there's more." Chaze took a deep breath.

"Don't tell me you're knocked up."

"Yes, I am."

"So you're keeping it." He stated disappointedly. "Do you plan on staying with my sister?"

"I can't just leave her like that Chaze. I have strong feelings for her. We just happen. I'm not trying to hurt anybody. But I want this child, and I want you to be a part of his or her life. I need you to respect my decision on this."

"So what are you saying? That you want me to be a father from the shadows?"

"No that's not what I'm saying. Look I have to go. I'll talk to you about this later." I hung up the phone and looked up to see Veronica standing in the doorway of our bedroom.

"Who was that?" Veronica asks calmly as she made her way onto the bed and straddled her legs around me from behind. She started massaging my shoulders.

"Don't start," Veronica.

"I haven't said anything. You're too stressed baby, let me calm you down." She began placing soft kisses on the back of my neck. Even though it was feeling good and I wanted to get down with her, I had to meet Juan to get the work. Not only that, but I felt like Veronica was playing me. She was the cause of some of this stress that I was experiencing. I pushed her away and jumped up from the bed. "I ain't got time for this shit right now. I got to go meet a man about a mule." She looked at me dejected—then she laid back on the bed with a smile that turned into hysterical laughter. Her body shook hard as her laughter resounded throughout the room. All I could do was look at her and think. "This bitch is truly crazy." She done lost her marbles, I didn't say a word. That's where I left her as I walked out on my way to meet Juan.

Maybe the stress and pressure of it all was too much for Veronica to handle and she was finally losing it. They say when a person goes insane, within their minds, they find their form of peace in insanities dreamland. I didn't have time to dwell on that situation. I needed my mind clear to take care of this business.

***

I jumped in my Range Rover and made a call to Jerf. I told him to meet me near the rental company with an untraceable car, phone and pistol. You never knew what might happen in these type of situations. So it was always best to stay prepared. After meeting up with Jerf and exchanging cars, we went our separate ways. Five minutes later he called.

"Look I know you're a big girl and all, you sure you don't need me to roll for back up?"

"Naw, this is Juan we are talking about, Uncle Alejandro's son."

"Yeah, I know who you are speaking of. The same mother fucker who has had a chip on his shoulder the size of the Hubert H. Humphrey Metrodome towards you."

"Man, that's old shit. With Juan, it was all a trust issue. Right now those issues have been put to rest."

"Aight, I just hope your trust issues don't get you put to rest," Jerf stated still not comfortable with me going alone.

"Jerf chill with that shit. You already know, I ain't trying to hear it."

"I know man and I'm sorry. Just be careful and call me if you need me. I'll be here."

"Okay cool."

"Ok I'm out," he said hanging up the phone.

As I coasted down the highway, I thought of all the people in my life and all the drama unfolding around them. It was always something. Always somebody with a private war to fight. I felt like one of the US soldiers being pulled from the US to help fight other country wars. When there were battles here at home that needed to be fought. I unconsciously turned on the radio. It tuned into an oldies soft rock station, and ironically a song by Phil Collins was just coming on. As it played, I could feel my grandmother's words tugging at my heart. I try to shake them off as I listened to the words of the song. "I can feel it...coming in the air tonight... oh Lord..." In my mind, body, and soul, I knew something was coming in the air tonight. I just didn't know what exactly. In my mind I visualized it to be me taking my rightful place on my throne in the kingdom in which I was about to create. *"Oh yes, I could feel it coming."* Coming in the air tonight, I thought as I smashed the pedal and accelerated down the highway. Headed to my tomorrows, while I left my yesterdays behind.

THE HIT

CHAPTER 25.

I arrived at the warehouse about 11:30 pm and started getting everything ready for the meet. I planned to drive the car that I was storing the drugs into the safe house myself. I was just getting ready to secure the building when my cell phone rang. I looked at the caller ID and saw that it was Veronica. She was starting to irritate me at this point. "What's up Veronica?"

"Nothing, where are you?"

"I'm out and about taking care of business."

"You probably with your bitch," she spat out.

"Look, I ain't got time for this shit."

"Well, what the fuck do you have time for? Because it sure isn't me, your damn dream woman."

"Look, Veronica " I started to say when I could have sworn that I had just heard one of the doors to the warehouse open. I paused, looked in the direction of the noise and listen for any more sounds.

"Keisha, Keisha, I know your ass hear me." Veronica screamed into the phone.

"Look, Veronica, I'm gone have to call you back."

"No your ass ain't, you gone talk to me now, she continued in her uproar. I heard a faint noise in the background as she spoke. It sounded familiar. Veronica where are you?" I asked

"Bitch don't try to switch this thing around on me. I'm out and taking care of business."

By this time she had worn on my last nerve, and I was ready to hang up. "Look I got to go. I'll holla at you later." I said hanging up in her face. I went back to securing the building. Once I finished, I sat and waited for Juan, but for some reason, I felt as if something was out of place. I couldn't put my finger on it, but I had a strong feeling that something was not right. Again I shook off the feeling that I felt tugging at my heart.

I saw the lights from Juan car shine through the windows. Seconds later I heard the horn blow three times signaling for me to roll up the garage doors. I hit the automatic switch and watched as the two cars pulled into the building. Juan was riding shotgun in a black S600 Benz with tinted windows. A white paneled van was following it.

Juan stepped out and greeted me with a smile and a nod.

"Are you ready to be rich and take over this city my friend?"

"As sure as shit stank and the sky is blue," I responded with a smile of my own.

"Are you alone or did you bring help for this?" he asked.

"Naw, it's just me. I'll be the only one with access to the product for now."

"Good, good. Well, let's get on with it. I have a flight to catch." Juan said as he gestured with his hand for the men in the white van to bring the work.

Two men stepped out of the van from the driver and passenger side—another two made their exit through the sliding side door. They all held guns in their hands and were looking around very cautiously. The driver of Juan car stayed put but was alert and watchful. One of Juan men retrieved six big black duffle bags from the van and was bringing them to the table where Juan and I were standing.

"Here you go, my friend," Juan said as the man set the bags down on the table. "There are fifty kilos in each bag, and this is only the first shipment. When you get things together as you want, there will be a weekly drop off of at least two hundred kilos and."

Juan words were cut short when four men came out from behind cars and work shelves inside the warehouse. They were holding AK 47 and an AR 15 assault rifles. "Get down mother fuckers." They screamed.

"Don't none of you bitches breathe or I'm gone ventilate your bitch asses with some hot ones." One of them threatened.

Even though these men wore a ski mask, you could tell they were young hood niggas. Even their clothing was hood with their oversized shirts and pants hanging off their asses. Shocked by all of this, I stood there frozen for a split second. But Juan and his men had upped their pistols immediately.

Aiming at the gun toting youngsters, Juan screamed at me. "What the fuck is this Kash?"

"Don't you fucking move!"

One of the gunmen forcefully gestured his gun towards Juan.

"Aye motherfucker. Put that goddamn gun down—before I blow your shit all over the floor."

Juan swung his pistol back towards the gunman, "No motherfucker you put your weapon down. You don't want to do this, my friend. It won't turn out pretty for you," Juan said with calmness.

"Nigga I'm holding a chopper on your bitch ass. It ain't gone turn out pretty for you." The gunman responded.

Hearing his response, I recognized his voice. It was Chaze, Veronica little brother. In disbelief, I cocked my head to the side in confusion and said Chaze? Man, what the fuck are you doing?

"Shut the fuck up," He screamed.

Juan was maneuvering his gun back and forth between both of us. "You know who this is Kash? What are you trying to pull here? Are you trying to get your woman's brother to jack me?"

"What the fuck are you doing Chaze?" I asked again.

"Bitch shut the fuck up. You know what time it is."

"Yes we do my friend," Juan said with a devilish grin.

He raised his left hand into the air—palm up then made a fist. The other three gunmen had their guns aimed at Juan men who were also aiming their weapons at the youngsters. The big man that was carrying the duffel bags still had two in his hands and stood frozen halfway between us and the van. As everyone pointed their guns at each other, the three youngsters were moving back and forth nervously from foot to foot. They were waiting to see what Chaze was going to do. You could see the agitation in their body languages when I called out Chaze's name.

Once again, I was in a situation that looked like a Mexican standoff. Only it was Columbians and me on one side and blacks on the other. And these young niggas were just as crazy as the Columbians. Things had quickly escalated to a place where I didn't want or needed them to be. When Juan raised his fist in the air, Chaze spoke, "What the fuck are you doing shawty? Ain't no black power fist going to save your burrito eating ass."

That's when I heard a shot and saw the flash of a gun coming from the backseat of Juan Benz. The bullet penetrated through the window seal and struck Chaze in the shoulder. All hell broke loose. Chaze goons pull their triggers, firing off at Juan men who were standing in front of the van. The one on the driver side was hit in the Stomach first then caught a hail of bullets. He fell dead into a bloody heap. The guy on the passenger side immediately fires his pistol, striking another youngster in the shoulder. Knocking him down and causing him to drop the AK-47 he was holding. The man holding a duffel bag roll to the ground pulled his pistol, shooting that youngster in the head. The impact blew the kid's brains out of the back of his head, and all over his friend—he ran for cover. Juan grab me and shoved me to the ground behind the table where the dope was. "I told you not to trust that little son of a bitch."

The three remaining goons had taken position behind some of the cars that were parked in the warehouse. One open fire on the Benz as the driver and backseat assassin tried to step out and join in on the action. They were met with a barrage of bullets that left them dead in the two open doors. Chaze had slid out of harm's way and was now hiding behind a car with his homey. He had exchanged his assault rifle for semi-automatic pistol and begin to fire our way. He then yelled, "*Kill that bitch who just kill Ray Ray!*" Immediately the other two did as they were told, concentrating all their fire on the transporter. He was out in the open. They left his body limp and riddled with slugs. Juan and I jumped into action and opened fire on them two, striking one of them in the leg.

"Chaze, I'm hit," he screamed in pain.

"Don't stop shooting," Chaze ordered.

By this time, Juan man on the passenger side had gone into the van and came out with a street sweeper. He opened fire on the two crouched behind the car. The shots were loud and devastating—they shook the entire room. The slugs fiercely tore through one of them, sending him flying through the air to a quick and horrible death. The partner who had been shot in the leg seeing his friend blown away let his emotions take over and out of anger he rose up from his crouched position. He stepped from behind the safety of the car and started walking down on Juan's man with a barrage of bullets thrusting from the AR 15. He struck Juan's' man several times before the clip was empty. His last mistake he would make. I raised up running in a full sprint and opened on him. He tried to reach for his pistol, but it was too late. I was on point with the bullets that I sent shattering through his chest and head. As I stood over the fallen gunmen for a split second, I heard my name being called,

"KASH!"

It was Juan trying to warn me. When I turned in response to hearing my name, there stood Chaze with a devilish grin on his face, aiming his pistol, which he immediately fired at me. I saw the flash from the gun, and it seems as if the world clicked in slow motion. That was the last thing I saw. I remember lying on the floor of the warehouse fighting to breathe. Chaze had shot me in the side of my neck. Juan was on the move towards Chaze before the second shot was fired. Luckily for me, that was his last shot. Juan had reached him and slapped him across the face with his pistol, leaving a spray of blood across the car that he was kneeled beside. Juan pistol whipped him until he was unconscious.

Running over to me, Juan kneeled down beside me to survey the extent of my injuries. I was lying there with blood gushing out of my neck and mouth. My eyes were rolling around in my head. I was gone. I didn't feel anything or even know what was going on.

"Kash, my friend, stay with me. Don't panic. You're going to be alright," Juan yelled—as he removed a pen and a sharp thumb knife from his pocket. He proceeded to take the pen lose, then cut a small incision into my throat. He inserted the pen into the incision and created an airway for me to breathe.

What few people didn't know about Juan, including myself was that he initially was supposed to be a doctor. Against his father wishes, he dropped out to help the family. He brutally murdered and carved up so many of the rival factions family they were ready to call it a truce. After patching me up, Juan tied Chaze up and placed him in the trunk of one of my rental cars. After which he got me to the nearest hospital. I went into emergency surgery fighting for my child, and I lives.

Juan called his people to clean up the mess in the warehouse and had his men take Chaze to a safe location. He called Michelle to come to the hospital to be with me. She in turn called Kaylin, who was on the first thing smoking to Atlanta when she got the news. My surgery was touch and go. They almost lost me a couple of times, but miraculously I pulled through. The doctors said if it weren't for the Tracheotomy that Juan had performed on me, I wouldn't have made it. So in essence, Juan had saved my life.

I was in ICU and Michelle was informed that the first 48 hours were critical. It would depend on how I responded to the surgery to know if I would survive or not.

Meanwhile, Juan had taken his torture tools to Chaze to find out how he knew about the location and time of the meet. We both already knew, but he wanted to hear it. It didn't take long to get the information he wanted. After placing small incisions all over the boy's body, then soaking them in alcohol. In two hours Chaze was spilling his guts like a snitch on the stand. He told Juan that his sister had listened in on our conversation the night he had met me at the apartment. He explained that she was mad because I had gotten pregnant. Veronica felt betrayed, so she set up the jack. Veronica had called me while I was in the warehouse and did so as a distraction. She was watching outside a window. She had supplied them with a key that she had gotten duplicated while I was sleeping earlier that morning. I had the devil in my own house and knew it. I just didn't listen to my gut. I knew she was a vindictive woman, but I had no idea just how deep her treachery went. She was a woman who I loved and trusted.

After Chaze had finished spilling his guts about the attempted jacking, Juan obliged him by spilling his guts all over the floor by slicing his stomach open with a scalpel. By the time Juan filled Kaylin and Michelle in on the situation. Veronica had disappeared. It made her look that much guiltier. But she couldn't run forever.

After a few days, I pulled through. I was lucky once again to be alive, but what the doctors reviled to Kaylin was devastating. I was paralyzed on the right side of my body and would have breathing difficulties. Kaylin felt as if she had failed me again. I lay in the hospital bed, all I could think about was my past. The things that I had been through. All the trials and tribulations that I had endured throughout my young life. Trying to lay a foundation, but for what? Then it hit me. With all of the horrible things that I had done to get where I was trying to be. I was now in my own personal hell.

GOTCHA

CHAPTER 26.

Six months later I was finally able to go home. Which home was now back in Minnesota with Kaylin. After being shot and almost losing my life again, I knew it was time to settle down and get out the game. Kaylin had flipped the script and given her life to the Lord. My sister, the killer, the drug dealer was now a devoted Christian that went to church three times a week and twice on Sundays. Kaylin said her change is what grandma would have wanted. And after all that has happened. God was leading her into the direction of salvation.

Then there was my new born son. Due to my conditions, I had a scheduled C-section and he was delivered at 36 1/2 weeks. He was 5 pounds 19 1/1 inches. He was the spitting image of me. Kaymar Tione Jefferson, named after my father and Tia. I watched him grow. Sometimes he would approach me and look me in my eyes. With the same eyes, face, and smile I had at his age. With a look of confusion, I'm sure he wondered why I never walked or talked much like everyone else. I was being tortured. I would never be able to play with my son as a normal mother would. I was just blessed to be able to touch him. This was my hell. All because I was trying to make a come up.

A year after Tione was born, Uncle Alejandro and Juan surprised me by showing up to Tione's birthday party. Everyone was there, even Ashley and Da'Kwon showed up.

Sitting in the living room in my wheelchair, Juan and Uncle Alejandro came and sat next to me on the couch. Alejandro leaned over and whispered in my ear. Kash, I have located the bitch that has caused you these troubles. I would like to know what you want me to do. If you want retribution, let me know. As I sat there, I thought about the love I had for her at one time. Then I questioned whether she ever loved me. I thought about what she did. What she did to my family and loved ones. What she did to my son. I looked towards Uncle Alejandro with tears of hurt and anger in my eyes—rendering my decision and the fate of Veronica. In a quiet whispered, I struggled to let the words roll off my tongue.

"Delete...that...hoe," I said in between deep breaths. Uncle Alejandro stood up and smiled. "Well then, it's settled."

Kaylin and Michelle walked in from outside. "He wants it done," Uncle Alejandro said in joy.

"Good," Michelle said.

"Now that leaves the question, will this be personal or for hire?" Uncle Alejandro inquired.

"Personal," Michelle responded. Since Kaylin has given her life to the Lord—I would like to do it.

Uncle Alejandro protested, Michelle you never traveled down this road before.

"Then who?" Kaylin ask?

Juan walked over to the front door and opened it. When he stepped away from the door, Ashley walked in followed by another woman with a black hooded silk blouse on. The hood was pulled down over her head so that her face was hidden. From the way this lady walked, you could tell that she was in good shape.

"This is the one who will carry out the deed." Uncle Alejandro said with a smile. "Guess who's back!" the woman sang as she lifted her hands to the hood and pulled it back to reveal her face. An incredible surprise, it was beautiful, slimmed down Alexis. I couldn't believe my eyes. She opened her arms to accept a round of hugs and a barrage of questions about how she got out of prison.

"Wait, wait. Dang, can a bitch get in the door first? I will answer all y'all question's but let me see my best friend"

Alexis walked over shaking her head as a tear rolled down her cheek. She grabbed my left hand and squeezed it. Then leaned down over me and placed a gentle kiss on my lips. Her mouth moved close to my ear, "Hey babe. I'm here now. I love you, and I'm sorry I wasn't there to have your back. But I'm gonna get revenge for you." She stood up and wiped the tears from my eyes. We shared a stare of regret n both our ends. "Okay, now I'll answer ya'll questions."

"So what happened? How did you get out?" Kaylin asked.

"Yeah, and I want to know why your ass didn't let us know." Michelle added. "You didn't even tell me at the visit last week."

"Well, I got out because my appeal came through. Thanks to Uncle Alejandro," Alexis told them.

"I have a few friends in high places who pulled a few strings. It wasn't like I had to bribe anyone because she was wrongfully convicted anyway. The judge should have never struck down the motion to allow the video surveillance tapes from the hotel and the shopping center into evidence. I put pressure on my people to speed up the process." Uncle Alejandro explained.

"Yes, you did. I thank you and love you for that. Now as far as why I didn't called no one and let them know. Well, we wanted to surprise you. I wanted this day to be special. Juan got news on the day of my release the location of Veronica, which is California."

"She thought she could hide right up under our noses." Juan voiced.

"She knew that we all would look for her in Atlanta and in Minnesota. Eventually, she would run out of money and would have to get a job. She's at Applebee's as a server. My friend Keisha," Juan said looking at me.

I acknowledged his statement with a weak wave of my left hand. After singing Happy Birthday to Tione. We got down to business. Uncle Alejandro explained that Alexis would travel to California tomorrow and the deed will be done. We have her daily routine and access to her apartment. It should be easy as pie. All weapons will be waiting for you when you get there.

"Gotcha bitch." Alexis grinned.

"Now everybody, let's get back to the party. There is life to celebrate," Uncle Alejandro exclaimed. As everyone went outside to the back, Michelle pulled Alexis by the hand.

"What's up babe?" Alexis questioned.

Michelle approached her staring directly in the eyes, holding her hand, she whispered. "I'm going with you to Cali." She said.

"Bitch are you crazy? You're staying right here. You heard what Uncle Alejandro said."

"I don't give a Fuck," Michelle said in a high pitched whisper.

"Come on Michelle, don't put me in this position." Alexis begged.

"Bitch this is my heart and the woman I love. Let me do this with you please." She pleaded desperately.

They stared at each other in silence—faces just inches apart. I tapped my finger and broke their stare. With my finger, I signal for them to come close and in a raspy whisper, I said "let her" Tears started to fill my eyes. At this point, I knew Michelle was about to pass the point of no return and that she would never be the same. I shed tears for the unconditional love and true loyalty that they both had for me. Alright, Alexis agreed. Pulling Michelle into her arms and planting a soft kiss on her lips. Michelle returned the gesture and savored the familiar taste of Alexi's sweet tongue. After pulling apart, they both walked to me and kissed me on both cheeks at the same time. I closed my eyes tight, praying that I would open them and this would all be a nightmare. I would wake up in the apartment in Atlanta on the day of the deal and be able to make a better decision than the one I had.

DELETE

CHAPTER 27.

Veronica returned to her apartment after a long day of work from Applebee's. Having to deal with many hungry and drunk folks who tipped little. Dropping her bag on the sofa, she undressed all the way to the bathroom leaving a trail of close behind her. She let out a deep sigh when she made it to the shower. Her feet were killing her. She turned on the water and adjusted it as hot as she could stand it. Entering the shower, Veronica let the hot water run down her body. Hoping it would ease some of the tension of the day. As she savored the feeling of the jetting spray caressing her body, she smiled at the thought of her pain. She really couldn't complain. It was either this life or death Knowing that Keisha people were out searching for her, she had to sacrifice her usual comforts in life.

Veronica also had to deal with her torn feelings that she felt because of the loss of her only brother and the way she had done Keisha. She knew her brother wouldn't make it out alive. Besides, he slept with Keisha and knocked her up, and Keisha didn't provide her with money in which to live. She wasn't all the much torn over the situation. It was all Keisha's fault.

Quickly as her face was turned up in anger, it quickly changed into a smile. The married man that she met who had come through with his family—He slipped her his cell phone number and told her to call him. She was thinking of how much she could juice him for, but her thoughts were interrupted by a noise in the bathroom.

Veronica quickly turned the water off and peeked out the shower door. She was startled as she peered into the steam filled room and saw a figure perched up on the edge of the sink.

"Hey bitch, bring your stank ass out of the shower before I come in there and get you." Alexis order with deadly hostility in her voice.

As the steamed cleared from her line of sight, Veronica saw that it was Alexis sitting there. She was holding a pistol with a silencer attached to the end of it.

Veronica's thoughts raced and her heart pound in her chest as she hesitated to step out of the shower. "Where the hell did Alexis come from? I thought she was locked up. I've heard a lot of stories about her. This crazy bitch is going to kill me for what I did to Keisha. *Oh God, help me please.*" Was the last thought to go through her mind before Alexis snatched her by the hair. Viciously slapped her with the pistol and threw her down to the floor. "Bitch I said get the fuck out the shower!"

"Please, please, please, don't kill me!" Veronica cried in pain holding the side of her now swollen face.

"Bitch you kind of fine," Alexis said in a soft tone as she gazed down at her naked body. Alexis smiled, leveling the pistol on Veronica.

Lost for words, she didn't know what to do—thinking maybe she could get away.

"Get up and get to moving bitch."

Veronica slowly rose to her feet and started out of the bathroom faking a limp with Alexis right behind her. As soon as she made it out the bathroom, she swiftly kicked the bathroom door back into Alexis and made a run for it. The impact of the door caught Alexis off guard and knocked her backward. She stepped into a puddle of water in front of the shower and slipped losing her balance, she slightly fell back onto the toilet. Giving Veronica the time she needed to break the front door. Alexis pushed up with the swiftness of a cat and bolted through the bathroom door.

Veronica made it down the hallway and entered the living room, moving with the speed of lightning. Her bare feet smacked the floor as her naked body ran in fear. Her adrenaline was pumping. She saw the front door and could taste freedom and safety. A step away from the door, out of nowhere, Veronica felt a gut wrenching pain explode in her stomach. The blow doubled her over and instantly sent her to her knees. She couldn't find the breath to scream. Moaning and gasping for air, Veronica looked up to see somebody dress in all black wearing a ski mask and holding a t-ball bat. They removed their mask and it shocked Veronica to see that is was Michelle hiding behind the mask

"Going somewhere bitch?" Michelle asked her with a devilish grin, by this time, Alexis had made it down the hall. She ran over to Veronica, grabbed her by her hair and slapped the shit out of her. "If you try that shit again. I'll make you suffer before I kill your stinking ass."

"Fuck all this talking shit, let's do this hoe in and be done with it." Michelle said historically waving her gun in the air.

"I thought you said to wait and let you do it?"

"I did."

"Well?"

Snatching the gun from Alexis, Michelle positioned herself behind Veronica and held the gun to her head.

"Wait, Wait!" Veronica petitioned. "Please don't kill me, Keisha wouldn't want you to do this, she begged rapidly."

Michelle paused, listening to Veronica words. Alexis was sick and tired of Veronica's mouth. To show her growing impatience, she let out a big sigh, just as Michelle leaned down to whisper in Veronica's ear.

"Bitch Keisha sent me to kill you. She gave the order." Pressing the muzzle tighter to her head, "This is for Keisha," Michelle said squeezing the trigger. The bullet exploded through Veronica's head killing her instantly. Michelle gazed at her body for a moment, then Alexis took the gun from her and shot her twice more. Then they both exited the apartment as quietly as they came. Walking out the back door of the complex into an ally. They climbed into a black Mercedes Benz and the driver pulled off into the darkness.

Acknowledgment

Every day is a blessing from the Lord. So first and foremost I thank the Lord for this wild imagination that has allowed me to share with you all what runs through this mind of mine. I have been writing for several years and many stories have been created. Yet Kash is the one that made it to print. I hope you all have enjoyed it and I thank you all for the love and support.

I want to thank the many people who saw me through this book and to all those who provided support. I want to give a special thank you to Chyrell for her hard work in assisting me in many chapters. I would had not gotten this done in a timely matter without you. My co-worker who offered her advice as well. To all those who have been a part of my upbringing. From 31st and 1st avenue South, till this day. You all have shaped me into the woman I am.

And I'm not sorry I married the south side enemy

Even if the whole world would be against my man,
I would stand behind his back and pass the bullets! ~ Brigitte Nicole

Nobody has been more important to me in the pursuit of this project than my children. No matter what anyone tells you, if you put your mind to it, you can accomplish anything.

ABOUT THE AUTHOR

Kimberly Fields is an author, professional hairstylist, and enthusiastic freelance writer. She has been hired to write for EGL: Everything Girls Love Magazine for credit work. She holds an A.A.S. degree in Criminal Justice. Born in the land of ten thousand Lakes, Minneapolis, MN, she is devoted to serving her urban community and loves to help people. She is happily married and continues reside in the beautiful city of Minneapolis, Minnesota. At her leisure time, she bakes, writes, showcases her terrific arts & crafts skills, and loves to spend quality time with her family. Her charisma and passion shows through her work and life.

You can contact Kimberly via email:

womenalty@gmail.com